JAKE WHITTAKER, P.I.

BY
DIANE JOHNSON

Jake Whittaker, P.I.
Copyright © 2020 Diane Johnson

All rights reserved. No part of this book may be reproduced in any form or by any electronic or mechanical means, including information storage and retrieval systems, without written permission from the author, except in the case of a reviewer, who may quote brief passages embodied in critical articles or in a review.

This is a work of fiction. Names, characters, places, and incidents either are the product of the author's imagination or are used fictitiously, and any resemblance to actual persons, living or dead, events, or locales is entirely coincidental.

Cover design by Tatiana Fernandez
Interior design by Brian Schwartz

Published by Wise Media Group

ISBN: 978-1629671673
Library of Congress Control Number: 2019918772

v125

CHAPTER 1
I KID YOU NOT

She wasn't cute, she wasn't ugly. She didn't look confident, she didn't look scared. She was maybe ten years old, with a short, faded dress over baggy tights. Looking into her big eyes, there were two things I was sure of: She had problems, and I don't deal with kids.

It was late on a summer night as she stood in the doorway of my office, first staring at me and then at the lettering on the door that said "Jake Whittaker, Private Investigations." I stared back, willing her to disappear.

She closed the door and moved toward my desk. "Are you Jake Whittaker?"

"Yeah."

"They said in the deli you might be able to help me."

Oh boy! "Look, kid," I said, "I don't work for free. I cost more an hour than your whole year's allowance."

Damn if she didn't burst out crying. She just stood there with shaking shoulders and tears dripping on the floor. She bobbed around, shifting her legs up and down, one at a time. A strand of dark hair escaped from the rubber band at the back of her neck. Her thin cheeks were pale, and she looked tired and hungry. Now she looked more ugly than cute and more scared than confident.

Then I sucker-punched myself by saying, "Okay, let's talk about it." I pointed to the torn seat on the client chair and got up to search through the debris on top of the file cabinet. When your office is also your home, stuff piles on top of stuff.

"I have Cokes here somewhere," I said. A forgotten box of donuts was hiding the Cokes, but I resurrected a couple of cans. They weren't cold and were probably well past their "best by" date. "In case you're hungry," I said, "if you can stomach warm Cokes and three-day old donuts . . .." I set the food between us.

She made short work of two donuts before she settled back in the chair, ready to tell me things I was sure I didn't want to hear. Kids are beyond my understanding. I never was a child myself. I was born at age ten, and I've been struggling ever since to learn everything I should have known before kindergarten.

"What's your name, sweetheart?"

"Cora Lee Sinclair, and I'm not your sweetheart."

Good grief, a precocious feminist. "Okay, I'm sorry, Cora Lee. What are you, ten? Twelve?"

"I'm eight and about to start third grade."

"So what's your problem?"

"My mom's missing."

"What do the police say?"

"I haven't told them."

I was reaching for the phone when she screamed, "Noooo!"

My hand stopped midair. I still wanted her gone, but now I was curious, too. I let the phone be and said, "Maybe you'd better tell me what's going on."

For the next ten minutes I listened to her tale, punctuated by sniffles, wide eyes, and snatches of both smiles and tears. Cora Lee's father was dead, and she and her mother were escaping an abusive boyfriend. Trying to save first-and-last for an apartment, they lived in their car and ate leftover food from the coffee shop where her mother was a waitress.

They'd parked on my street late yesterday before her mother left to walk to work. "She never came back," Cora Lee finished.

"You mean you were alone in the car last night?"

Cora Lee nodded, tears brimming.

"Then you need the police to help you. They can find your Mama."

Her head shook violently. "If they find out we're living in the car, Mama says they'll take me away from her." Her eyes were swimming, pleading. "You have to find her, Mr. Whittaker."

Shit! Now she was sucker punching me with feminine wiles—and it was working. I'm not sure what came out of my mouth next, except that it sounded more soothing than I care to recall and more confident than any sane person would believe. I found myself filling up my pocket notebook with her answers to my questions, and I never mentioned a word about a fee.

But now I had another problem. Just allowing this kid into my office without another adult present was asking for trouble. I started thinking out loud. "Well, you can't stay another night in the car by yourself, but what am I going to do with you? You sure can't stay here with me. It wouldn't be right." I didn't mention that I could end up in jail.

She glanced toward the window, fear covering her face, like she could see the darkness beyond the dirty windows. "It's so dark out there," she said.

I looked at my watch and realized the whole city was already asleep or closed up for the night. The next words that came out of my mouth shocked even me. "Well," I drawled, "maybe you can stay here just one night, but *just one*. Got that?"

"Oh, thank you, thank you!" she said, looking around my one-room office, taking in the clutter, the hot plate on a small table, and the couch with its pillow and blanket shoved to one end.

"I won't be any trouble, honest I won't," she said. "I have my own blanket and pillow in the car." She pointed to a corner beside the file cabinet. "I'll make my bed over there." A grin appeared on her face as she added, "And I like donuts a whole lot."

What was there not to like about the kid? My mind was already upgrading my act to some canned chili among my assortment, and maybe Egg McMuffins in the morning. Right now we both needed more than donuts.

So she cooked while I found a couple of spoons to wipe off. She managed the can opener like she'd been doing it all her life and set both cans of chili directly on the hotplate. She stirred as it heated up. When the steam looked right, we wrapped the hot cans in towels and spooned chili from can to mouth, ignoring the burned beans at the bottom. She had a good appetite for a skinny little kid. I ate my can while making excuses to myself.

I walked her back to her mother's car and watched her pull a key on a chain from under the neckline of her dress. While I stood guard, she opened the car door and gathered up what she needed.

Back at the office I sacked out on the couch fully dressed except for shoes. Cora Lee changed into flannel pajamas in the women's room down the hall. Dreamland escaped me for a long while as my mind refused to give me any peace. *Jake Whittaker, this isn't smart!* a small voice kept whispering in my head. I told my guardian angel to shut up and finally slept with my head under the blanket.

The next morning we wolfed down deli egg sandwiches before going to the diner where her mother worked.

The Hot Cup isn't that far from my place. It's a typical coffee shop, complete with booths, counter stools, and a chalkboard with the day's specials, but it's a place that won't run a tab, so it doesn't get much of my business. It was midmorning, and only a few customers were deciding between breakfast and lunch.

A waitress appeared as soon as we walked in. She wore one of those mustard-colored uniforms with the requisite little white apron. Her curly hair was unbelievably blonde, with a couple of tresses hanging down as companions with big, dangly earrings. Her smile was believable, though. She ran up and put an arm loosely around Cora Lee. "Where's your mom?" she said.

"She's gone, Donna," Cora Lee said. She nodded toward me. "Mr. Whittaker's gonna find her."

I pulled out a business card for the waitress and squatted to talk to Cora Lee. "Listen, honey, you wait for me over there in that booth. I need to talk to Donna." Cora Lee gave me a look that said she wasn't sure about what I was going to do, but she left me and slid into a booth. She was right; I didn't know what I was gonna do. I wagged my head at Donna and settled into a stool at the counter.

Donna went behind the counter and got Cora Lee a glass of milk before she poured a mug of coffee and set it in front of me. "On the house," she said. Then neither of us said anything more until I'd torn into three packets of sugar and stirred them into the mug. I looked up at Donna and said, "What do you know about Cora Lee's Mama?"

"Loretta's a damn good worker, I can tell you that. This was her first job as a waitress, but she had to have been one in another life, because she's was that good."

"Was?" I said. "You know something I don't?"

She glanced at Cora Lee before bending down and leaning both arms on the counter. "I mean 'was' as in she don't work here anymore. When she cut out on one shift and didn't show for the next one, the boss let her go—only she don't know it yet. She hasn't been back since."

"How well do you know her?"

This time I got a shrug. "I know she and Cora Lee were living out of her car. I know she was running from a friggin' maniac named Billy Miller who treated her like a punching bag." Her head nodded toward Cora Lee. "Loretta said Cora Lee was seeing too much of it, so they cut out, hoping Billy would leave them alone."

"Would Loretta go off and leave Cora Lee?"

"Hell no! She really loves that kid." Donna reached for a damp cloth and began to wipe an already-clean counter. "Loretta got a call early in her shift. I think it was from Billy. She cut out faster than a speeding train, and I haven't seen her since."

I closed my eyes for a moment in a futile attempt to block out the seamy side of life I was imagining.

Finally I looked up at Donna. "You obviously like Cora Lee," I said. Then I looked back down at my coffee and added, "I think we'd both hate to see the authorities get their hands on her before I find her mother." I said that like I actually thought I was actually — actually — going to look for and find Loretta. In a low voice I said, "She can't stay with me..."

My coffee cup was half drained before Donna said, "Well... maybe Cora Lee could stay with me tonight . . . if you bring her here at the end of my shift."

Bingo! I jumped on that suggestion with both feet. "That's great! What time do you get off?"

She looked resigned as she gave me a time. "This is for one night only, understand?" she said.

I smiled at her and added, "And don't worry, I'll pick her up here in the morning." A look of agreement passed between the two of us.

"Anything I need to know to help me track down Loretta? And probably Billy?"

"I don't know where he lives. He'll be wherever the action is, where he can be a player without being a payer. With Billy you better watch your back." She was biting her lower lip. "And put a fist in his face for me, will ya?"

She went to retrieve dirty dishes from the other end of the counter, so I figured out I should move on. The sooner I did something about finding Loretta, the sooner I'd get rid of Cora Lee. Kids never have been my style. And here I was about to take her with me while on a hunt with the improbable.

I left a dollar on the counter anyway and went to explain to Cora Lee that I'd bring her back later to spend the night with Donna. "We'll find my Mama before then," she offered. She had more faith than I did. I didn't tell her that having a root canal or giving birth to an elephant might be easier than finding her Mama.

Cora Lee sat on the other end of my office couch while I explained that Billy might have found her mother and wouldn't let her go.

"So we make Billy give her back," she said.

"Whoa, it's not that easy." I wasn't about to mention that abused women stand a great chance of getting killed when they finally leave an abuser. For a nanosecond her face went blank before she turned away from me, pulled her legs up to her chest, and curled her body into a ball.

"Hey," I murmured, "I didn't say we couldn't do it. It's just gonna take some doing."

Before I could stop her, she threw her arms around my neck. "Thank you, Jake!" she said. Then she backed up to frown into my face. "But you need to shave first." I don't need to shave—or even put on a clean shirt—for most of the P.I. work I do, especially since I don't get a lot of clients. When I hit middle-age, I quit making demands on myself.

"You're right!" I said, untangling myself and getting up. I found a ten-dollar bill and held it out to her. "I'll shave while you get sandwiches from the deli next door. I'm starved."

The idea of food made her scamper. "Mustard only for me," I yelled as she headed for the door.

She turned to give me an impish smile. "Mustard on peanut butter and jelly?" she said.

I faked an evil-monster look and said, "On any kind of meat, you peanut butter-and-jelly freak!" She was skipping as the door swung shut behind her.

★★★

We were in my car, coming up on the last address where Cora Lee and her mother had lived with Billy. They had moved often when the rent was overdue, so we were running on hope. "Listen," I said, as I got out of the car, "you lock every door and keep out of sight. Under no circumstances are you to open up for anyone but me. Understand?"

"I told you I wouldn't. I'm not stupid, you know."

"I know, kid, I know."

It wasn't my week for smart decisions. I had no idea what I was going to do or say when I stepped into the lobby of an old motel converted into cheap sleeping rooms. The sign over the plywood desk said rooms were rented by the week or the month, supply your own towels. "Hello," I called out.

A matronly type appeared in the doorway behind the desk.

I smiled and said, "Which room is Billy Miller?"

"Gone," she said. "He left about a week ago. Owed me three weeks rent when he cut out in the middle of the night." She could imagine my next question. "And no, he didn't leave no forwarding address."

"He leave alone?"

"Far as I know. But the woman who used to live with him was back yesterday. She was asking after him, too."

"Yesterday? What'd you tell her?"

"Same thing I just told you. Who the hell cares where they go." With that she stepped back into her room and slammed the door in my face. I headed back to the car.

I didn't tell Cora Lee her Mama had gone looking for Billy without her. It was too much for her to understand. It was too much for me to understand, too. I wasn't even sure the woman looking for Billy was Cora Lee's Mama. At this point I wasn't even sure Billy hadn't dragged Loretta to another town where they could get lost. I didn't want to think about Loretta being dead.

We were digging into soft-shell tacos when I asked Cora Lee to tell me every place Billy hung out, every friend he might have.

"I don't know his friends," she said, "but he goes to the gym a lot when he can afford it," she said.

Oh great, I was chasing after someone with more muscles than I had. "How 'bout a job," I asked, "does Billy have a job?"

"He works sometimes at a place called The Hog Shop."

"Oh boy! That was a tough bar/pseudo-restaurant on the far west side that catered to bikers and scrapers looking to make a reputation in a fistfight. "What's Billy do there?" I said.

"He bounces."

It figured. Now I was sure to end up bleeding.

I left Cora Lee in the car at a strip mall a block from The Hog Shop. We had picked up some books from her car, and she settled into the floorboards of the back seat with all doors locked while I walked to the bar.

I tried to put on a swagger halfway between self-confidence and unthreatening as I pushed my way into the bowels of a bar that microwaved the only food some drunks ever got. It was dark and noisy inside, the kind of place that gums up your shoes with spilled beer and peanut shells. The muscle types wrapped in leather stared at me as I walked to the back of the place. The sloppy drunks didn't even see me. They were all present, the wild, the wooly, and the disgusting.

When I reached an office marked "Management, No Admittance," I knocked.

"Yeah?" a voice said. In my book that means "come in," so I did.

The sleaze ball behind a desk had a cocky face that advertised power without a hint of humility. He actually wore a vest over a T-shirt, making my plaid flannel shirt and wrinkled slacks feel positively formal. He took one look at me and said, "Who the hell are you?"

"Whittaker," I said, "as in I think you want to hear what I have to say."

He sneered like he'd heard it all before and said, "I doubt that." He studied me for a moment, like he didn't approve of plaid or wrinkles, then waved at the chair in front of him, saying, "Okay, I'll listen."

I sat down and started right in. "I need information on one of your employees. Billy Miller. Like where's he live?"

"What's it to you?"

"It's more of what's it to you. I figure this place can't stand up to a thorough investigation. The licensing board isn't going to take kindly to an employee with a felony conviction working in a bar." I was guessing Billy had a record—or one or two of his other employees—but sometimes a guess makes a good bluff.

He grabbed a gold pen and wiggled it rapidly between two fingers. "What's Miller supposed to have done?"

Instead of answering his question, I said, "Let's just say I'm a Good Samaritan willing to weed out the bad apples so you can stay legit."

He wasn't buying the Good Samaritan bit, but he wasn't willing to dismiss it either. The pen in his hand was still as he thought about it. Finally, with a shrug, he grabbed a page off his desk calendar, wrote on the back of it, and said, "Give this to my bookkeeper, second door on the right." I took the note and stood up. "And," he added, "I don't want to see your face in this place again." He studied me once more and let out a chuckle. "Piece of advice," he said. "Get lost before you get hurt."

"What? And miss the opportunity for you to pay for some bridge work I need anyway?" I left him staring at my back while I walked out with a fake macho I didn't really have.

The note got me Billy's latest address, and even his unit number, from the bookkeeper. Sure, the address could be bogus or outdated, but I was feeling like a lottery winner as Cora Lee and I headed back to The Hot Cup. Donna's shift was ending, and I needed to drop Cora Lee off. I promised to join them there in the morning for breakfast.

My next stop was a much-needed beer break at my own favorite place, Frank's Bar, where I washed down pretzels with beer until my stomach demanded something more. Frank was trying out a new sandwich grill that looked like a waffle iron without the dimples, so with a little sizzle and a little steam, I had a toasted jalapeno cheese sandwich and chips along with another tall foamy.

Early the next morning I was back at the coffee shop. My eyes were trying to stay open, and I was blaming the food from Frank's sandwich machine, not the beers or long hours I had stayed there.

Donna was too busy to look after the kid while she worked, but Cora Lee and I sat at the counter and shared a plate of donuts before we took off. Cora Lee had filled up her hollow leg and was giggling from a sugar buzz. I knew she was planning on seeing her mother by the end of the day, because she told me so. The cynic in me just stayed quiet.

The sun was playing King of the Hill as we headed out to the address I'd been given for Billy. Needless to say, it was a neighborhood a feral cat would avoid. If Billy was there, he was living in another defunct motel that had turned itself into sleeping rooms and then religiously avoided any maintenance.

"Lock the doors and stay down," I demanded as we parked at the curb just past the motel. "You know the drill."

I got a brilliant smile from her. "Go get my mom," she said.

As I searched for the right room, I knew the odds for finding Loretta were slim to none. But since we'd had a movie actor as President of the United States, maybe anything is possible! It was also possible that I could experience pain on this job, but the image of an eight-year-old face told me to risk it.

I got no response the first time I knocked on the door, so I pounded with my fist and thought I heard movement inside. "Billy?" I yelled.

The door opened and a burly predator-type, wearing only jockey shorts, filled up the entire doorway. He looked me over and said, "Who the hell are you?"

"Let me in and I'll explain," I said. I needed to see if Loretta was in there. His eyes told me I was merely a pesky fly, but he stepped back to let me in. No one else was in the bedroom, and a quick look through the open bathroom door told me Loretta wasn't there. When I turned back around, Billy was leaning against the outside door with his arms folded across his chest. I knew I was trapped.

"I'm looking for Loretta Sinclair," I said. "I'm Jake Whittaker, an investigator for Gregory, Gregory & McGregor, representing the estate of Ms. Sinclair's maternal grandmother." It was an old ploy, but I figured greed had a higher priority with Billy than common sense. If he took the bait, maybe Loretta was still alive. If not....

"Yeah, so?" he sneered.

"Finding Ms. Sinclair is important to the law firm. They can be very thankful for any help they get."

"You talking about thanking *me*, not you?"

"Of course."

"You mean like in real money?"

I nodded and he smiled for the first time. "How much we talkin' about?"

I shrugged. "I'm only the errand boy."

"Well, my knowledge don't come cheap."

My heart skipped a beat. Maybe Cora Lee's wishes could come true. "You know where she is?"

"I might."

"No problem," I said, "GG&McG will pay finder's expenses right out of the estate." I grinned and looked him up and down. "You look like a big expense to me."

He smiled again. "Damn straight. You can tell those shysters it'll cost two thousand bucks. Cash."

I shook my head. "They won't go for cash. You could take the money and run before we find Ms. Sinclair." I focused on his eyes and added, "Don't worry, they'll pay."

His face showed he was already spending the money, but his words showed he was also afraid of being stiffed. He shook his head. "No way," he said. "Cash only. After I find Loretta for them, I get paid pronto, on the spot." He hesitated for a moment and added, "And, mind you, I'm not saying I *know* where she is, but I might be able to locate her for the cash."

"They won't buy it that way. You'd have to go to their office for the cash."

He considered that. "They don't trust me; I don't trust them. I want a paper promising they'll pay. Their name printed on the page, all legit. They sign up front saying that when I give you Loretta, they'll pay the 2K as soon as I get to their office.

Give you Loretta? He did have her! "Of course," I said.

"I want it in writing today." He seemed to think about that for a minute and added, "Be here at seven thirty tonight."

I started to protest, but he cut me off. "I'm not saying nothin' more until my ass is covered." He stood aside and opened the door.

I didn't want him blindsiding me, so I turned to face him as I passed through the door and said, "I'll be back."

"See that you are," he said, as the door creaked shut behind me.

★★★

Cora Lee's face said it all as I unlocked the car doors and climbed in. "Not yet," I told her, "but I think he knows where she is."

She screwed up her face. "Make him tell, Jake!"

I couldn't imagine forcing Billy to do anything. But I could imagine the look on Cora Lee's face if and when she got her mother back. "We're going to see that he does tell us, Miss Priss," I said, "but we gotta do it with a special paper you and I are gonna take care of."

When the car started on the first try, I took it as a good omen and headed back to the office. My old Olivetti typewriter needed to spit out some legal words that would snow Billy.

There really is a law firm named Gregory, Gregory & McGregor. I'd once filched some letterhead from a secretary's desk when she took a bathroom break. It took two hours of composing and pecking at keys to get the job done, but Cora Lee agreed the final copy on GG&McG letterhead looked authentic. I couldn't help but wonder what would happen if Billy ever did show up at the law firm to capitalize on the bogus promise.

We had a late lunch of saltine crackers and some watery soup heated on the hotplate before we headed back to the motel. This time I wasn't worried about the possibility of absorbing punches.

This time I was wrong.

★★★

I was feeling lucky when I left Cora Lee in the car, but no one answered the door to Billy's room after I knocked a couple of times. What the hell? I couldn't imagine his passing up the chance to exhort two thousand bucks.

I fast-walked back to what had once been the motel office. The door was locked, but a sign said "Manager." No lobby in this place, just manager quarters and rows of separate rooms. I knocked loudly over the noise of a TV. "Come back after Wheel of Fortune," a voice called out.

"I'm not here to rent a room."

"Then don't come back at all."

"I'm looking for Billy Miller in room twelve," I yelled.

The door opened immediately. "Why the hell didn't you say so? Get in here." An older woman in an old bathrobe and pink fuzzy slippers waved me into the middle of a fireman's nightmare. Multiple appliances on a counter ganged up at the end of an extension cord headed for one wall outlet. If they were all turned on at the same time, lights would dim a block away before the fire started. Luckily, Vanna White was smiling from the TV, attached through a separate outlet where she could maintain her classy composure before the fire department could arrive.

The room was an efficiency apartment with the bare necessities, full of clutter. The bed in one corner had sheets dingier than week-old underwear. Only the Formica table had a couple of clear spots. She pointed for me to sit and handed me a slip of paper saying, "GIVE HER THE PAPER SAYING I'LL GET THE MONEY," with Billy's name scrawled at the bottom.

"Hey, my deal's with Billy. Where is he?"

"Where you couldn't show up with the police." Her smile told me Billy had given her the whole story.

I hadn't seen this coming. Angry with myself, I got up and walked over to the appliance counter to think, but I couldn't figure a way out. Finally I pulled the so-called agreement out of my pocket and passed it to her. She read it thoroughly and said, "Seems in order. I'll see that Billy gets it. Then he'll tell me what you want to know, you sign the paper, and I'll tell you. Come back in an hour."

"Oh no," I said. "I'm only dealing with Billy and right now. No Billy, no payment."

Greed got the best of her. She obviously had been promised a share of the payout. "Okay," she said, "but right now he ain't here. "Come back in an hour. Alone."

"I'm here now. I'll wait the hour here."

"No you won't.. Go bug someone else for an hour. And don't loiter in the parking lot. If Billy sees you out there, he'll cut out."

I shrugged and headed for the door. She was right behind me, holding out a hand. "Billy said you'd pay me now for being the middle man."

"Lady, this time you're out of luck. The deal is with Billy. He wants you paid, he can do it."

"Frigging cheapskate!" she yelled. I had already turned to leave and didn't see her punctuate the words with a fist zeroing in on one side of my face. Cartilage cracked in my nose, my eyes watered, and I was knocked backwards. Pushing sideways, I got ready for a second punch, but it never came. She stood her ground, daring me to retaliate. I really, really wanted to hit her back, but my own Mama taught me different. I couldn't do it. Instead, I brought a foot up and wiped out several knobs along the bottom of the TV before I got the hell out of there. My Mama wouldn't have wanted me to listen to what she screamed at me. I think the whole neighborhood had to put their hands over their ears.

I headed back to the car, feeling good in spite of my aching face, but I wasn't looking forward to going back into the lion's den when I came back.

★★★

Just as Donna's shift was ending, Cora Lee and I were back at The Hot Cup. Maybe it was my red face and tearing eyes that persuaded Donna to take Cora Lee for another night. Or maybe the clincher was when I tried to look noble and said, "Do you really want her sleeping at *my* place?"

As I drove back to the motel, I was fingering my nose, listening to it crack as I drove in and out of the streetlights, heading for what I knew would be trouble. I tried to assuage my fears by telling myself that at least Cora Lee was safe. All in all, this day wasn't going down in history as one of my better ones.

★★★

When Fuzzy Slippers opened the motel door, I held up both hands in a sign of surrender. One hand held a twenty-dollar bill. She plucked it from my fingers and stepped aside to let me in. I kept both her hands in sight until I'd put some distance between us. I started out with, "Sorry about the TV, but you most definitely should not have hit me."

She shrugged and said, "It still works."

She walked to the window and peeked through the curtains. Once she was sure I had come alone, she said, "He's next door in room two."

I left her standing there and knocked on the next door, stenciled with a fading 2. There he was, Scum Ball, dressed in dirty jeans with muscles bulging through a black T-shirt. I tried to keep focused on my need to find Cora Lee's Mama and away from my heart trying to jump out of my chest.

The bathroom door was open, and I could see we were alone. He wasted no time pulling out the agreement on GG&McG letterhead and offered me a pen. "You sign here where it says I found Loretta for you," he said.

I waved both hand up in front of me. "How dumb do you think I am? I'm not signing anything until I see Loretta, *alive and well!*"

"You think I killed her?"

"Did you?"

An evil chuckle burst out of him. "Maybe I should have. The stupid bitch can't follow simple orders."

"So where is she now?"

"Anywhere I want her to be, so long as she thinks I might have her kid."

My face must have shown my disgust. "She thinks you kidnapped Cora Lee? That's how you got her to come back and stay with you?" He shrugged, and the pieces began to fall in place. "But you don't have Cora Lee, do you?" I was sorry the minute I said it.

He grinned. "No, but I will. I bet Donna knows where she is."

I didn't want to think what I was thinking. I needed to know where Loretta was and then get Cora Lee out of Donna's place.

Trying to refocus his thoughts on greed, I said, "The minute I see Loretta, I'll sign the paper."

He wagged his head at me to follow him as he headed out the door and walked a few yards under the motel overhang. I followed him into another motel room. The woman lying on top of the bed had a badly bruised face and looked like she'd been sleeping in her street clothes. When I took a step toward her, her eyes showed fear. She backed herself deeper into the bed. I put both palms up in the air to let her know I wasn't going to come any closer. As gently as I could, I said, "You Loretta Sinclair?" She nodded.

My head cocked to one side, and my voice was still gentle. "What color is your daughter's pillowcase?"

"Yellow," she whispered.

She was Cora Lee's Mama all right. "Okay," I said to Billy, "I'll sign the friggin' paper. You'll get your thirty silver coins."

"You mean two thousand."

"Yeah, two thousand."

He was grinning from ear to ear as he thrust the paper at me with a pen. I scribbled my name, held it out, and watched it disappear into his pocket. "She's all yours," he said. I moved a couple steps closer to Loretta, and her face contorted back into fear. Good grief, did she think I was a John that Billy was forcing on her? With my eyes on her face, I opened my mouth to protest, but a sudden, all-consuming pain plowed into the back of my head as I went down for the count. Sucker punched again.

Loretta was rubbing a cool cloth across my forehead when I pushed through a daddy of a headache and opened my eyes. "Whittaker," I mumbled, trying to remember who I was.

"I know," she said. "I found a business card in your pocket. Why were you asking about Cora Lee?"

Cora Lee! Damn. Billy was about to take her!

I stumbled to my feet as fast as my head would allow, staggering only slightly. "How long have I been out?"

"Maybe ten or fifteen minutes."

"Damn, we gotta move! Cora Lee's at Donna's place. Billy didn't have her before, but I guarantee he's headed there to get her now." The fear was back in her face. "I'm a little shaky," I said. "Think you can drive?"

When she nodded, I tossed her my keys.

Donna lived in a low-rent building where tempers voiced in other apartments were tolerated, and even outright screams might be ignored. Loretta pulled the car keys, and we took off running. "Upstairs," she said. By this time my head had cleared, and my limbs were steady again, so we took the stairs two at a time. In the dim overhead light, she pointed to a door on the second floor. I stepped in front of her, holding a finger to my mouth to keep her quiet while I put one ear to the door.

Nothing. Maybe Billy hadn't found Donna's place yet.

I motioned for her to step into the shadows before pounding on the door and calling out, "Wake up, Donna. It's Jake Whittaker." There was only silence.

I pounded again. For a moment I thought I heard something on the other side of the door, but it was the door to my left that opened. A guy in boxer shorts stood in the doorway and yelled, "Donna, let the friggin' asshole in so the rest of us can get some sleep!" Then he looked at me. "If it don't stay quiet out here, I'm callin' the cops. That's your one and only warning." Satisfied he'd told everyone off, he slammed the door.

This time my knock was softer but still insistent. I watched the doorknob turn and the door crack open. Finally. Even in that poor light I could see the swelling on Donna's face and the scared look in her eyes. I knew Billy was right behind the door. Gall rose up from the depths of my stomach, and I fought to keep it from erupting.

"Come back tomorrow, Mr. Whittaker. We're sleeping," she whispered.

"Okay," I said, but then I jerked her into the hallway, handing her off to Loretta, and propelled myself into the room. Billy was pushed back into the wall behind the door, but he recovered fast enough to slam the door behind me.

What I saw next almost brought me to my virtual knees. There was Cora Lee, sitting on the edge of a chair in front of a small coffee table, staring mutely into space, trying to escape from reality. I doubt she even knew I was in the room. She obviously had seen Billy beating Donna, but Cora Lee's clothes told me he probably hadn't touched her. I said a silent prayer of thanks before turning back to Billy.

He seemed satisfied to stand between me and the door, watching me take in what had probably happened, so I focused on Cora Lee. Swallowing a large hunk of my anger, I sat on the coffee table in front of her. "Sweetheart?" I said.

She didn't look at me.

"Cora Lee, I found your Mama."

Her eyes still didn't quite focus, but she turned to face me. "Mama?"

"Yes, you and I are going to go where she is."

"Like hell you are!" Billy yelled.

That did it. Full-blown anger flooded over me. I wanted him gone. I wanted him punished.

I wanted him dead.

A groan escaped from my mouth as I stood up, bringing the coffee table up over my head. I turned toward Billy, wanting to smash it into his head, but instead I slammed it into the wall that connected with the angry neighbor's place. It was very loud and very satisfying. I brought the table back over my head again and smashed it into the wall again, and then again and again.

When I stopped, I realized I had surprised myself as well as Billy. He said, "What the hell you do that for?"

Before I could answer, a voice yelled through the wall. "That did it. I just called the cops!"

"You're busted, Billy," I said. "You'll be walking out of here in handcuffs." I watched his face take it in, figuring his odds. Fight or flight. He decided on flight. The devil would envy the look he gave me as he headed out the door.

I let him go and listened to his heavy footsteps running down the stairs. There was only silence for a moment or two before a siren sounded nearby. I hoped they were in time to catch Billy running from the building

I didn't move; Cora Lee didn't move.

Then Loretta's shadow appeared in the doorway, with Donna right behind her. "Cora Lee?" Loretta whispered.

The real world came back to those eight-year-old eyes. "Mama!" she yelled, as she flew into Loretta's arms.

Wow! If anyone thinks I didn't get paid for this job, they didn't see the look on Cora Lee's face when she saw her Mama.

I could mark this case "paid in full."

CHAPTER 2
A CLEAN BREAK

The need for a real shower kicks in after about the sixth sponge bath. Since my P.I. office is also my home and the only running water is from the men's room down the hall, it isn't often enough I can turn into a scrubbed-up Prince Charming. I was feeling like an unclean, muddy-looking frog looking for a metamorphosis.

Cora Lee was back with her Mama, and my body was rested and the cartilage in my nose no longer cracked. With the case of Cora Lee's missing Mama closed, I figured I wouldn't be seeing Cora Lee again. Never seeing her again was okay, of course, because kids aren't my thing, even if one of them happened to be eight-going-on-eighteen. I work alone; I like it that way. Yeah, I work alone.

It was early morning as I sprinted through a downpour after having to park two blocks from an uptown address I'd been given over the phone. I was going to Mrs. Jameson's apartment because my second-floor office is not wheelchair friendly. She'd called with a problem about a niece, I needed the money badly, and the possibility of a new case pushed Cora Lee and her mother Loretta out of my mind.

There was a buzzer system to keep out the unwanted at the apartment complex, and I was buzzed in right away. Mrs.

Jameson was waiting for me at her open door. She reminded me of my Grandma, with a flowing pants suit that looked more like a long skirt and hair that didn't dare get out of place. The picture became complete when I saw a plate of cookies on a table in front of a flowered sofa. It was a comfortable place with wide spaces between groups of furniture, leaving room for her wheelchair to glide around easily.

She looked directly at me and said, "Welcome Mr. Whittaker. Please sit down." She wheeled toward the sofa and pointed me to a chair. Then she looked back at me, seeing how much the rain had had its way with me. She smiled and said, "Mr. Whittaker, it looks like the rain got the best of you. The coffee pot's slow, so if you want to use my shower, it's through that door right there." I hesitated. "Go on, Mr. Whittaker, go for it. The cookies and coffee can wait." She probably saw me weaken. "Set the shower stool out on the rug and grab any towel you see." She matched the smile that appeared on my face. "Meet you back here in about fifteen minutes," she said, "okay?" There was hospitality in her voice with just a speck of sadness. I think I fell in love instantly, but I headed to the bathroom.

Fifteen satisfying minutes later, it was a clean but slightly damp Prince Charming who sat before her with a cookie and a coffee mug balanced on one knee. "Tell me about your niece," I began. "What's the problem?"

"She was murdered four weeks ago. Anita's no-good boyfriend found her dead with an empty, unmarked medicine vial in her hand."

"Sounds like suicide or accidental death, not murder."

She made a noise of disgust. "So the police say. The boyfriend said she was despondent and depressed and must have taken too many pills accidentally—or on purpose. I told them she had no reason to be despondent and, besides, the police never found any pharmacy that filled a sleeping pill prescription for her. I told them she was healthy and took care of herself, that she had no reason to take any pills."

The room was quiet for a moment as a determined look spread across her face. "She was murdered," she said. "I know she was."

"What's the boyfriend say?"

"Says she was pretty broken up after he'd called it quits the night before. Says he found her dead the next day when he came back to get his leather jacket."

"What do the police say?"

"They wrote it up as a suicide."

"No autopsy?"

She wheeled her chair back a few inches as though she didn't want to face something. "Oh yeah," she said. "There were barbiturates in her system. Enough to kill her. Cops took the easy way out, closed the case, and went on to other things."

"What is it you want me to do?"

"Damn it, I want you to find her killer."

I try not to deal with murder cases. It raises goose bumps and appalling visions of bullets or knives. But I fought with myself inwardly. Not only did I have a flat wallet after feeding Cora Lee donuts and getting no fee, but surely a hot shower was worth at least a few innocent interviews.

She agreed it was a long shot to find a killer, but she nodded her head when I quoted my hourly rate and wrote a small check upfront. Then she gave me enough info to fill several pages of my pocket notebook. When I left her I didn't feel very hopeful, but I did feel cleaner.

The rain had become mist when I got to the boyfriend's midtown address, a walkup over a place called Fisher's Pharmacy with a display of designer condoms in a window. Ah memories.

I knocked at the door. Boyfriend answered but held a foot against the other side of the door, peering out at me like he was afraid I'd shoulder my way in. His eyes were glazed and the pupils dilated. I braced a foot on my side of the door and said, "Kevin O'Brien?"

"Yeah. Who's asking?"

"Name's Jake Whittaker. Mrs. Jameson said you'd be willing to talk to me about Anita."

"Well, the old lady's wrong, man." We both heard the noise behind him. He looked back over his shoulder for a second and told me, "This ain't a good time."

"Just give me a second, okay? Tell me what you saw when you found Anita."

"Look, I've told you cops three times already. I've said all I'm gonna say without having a lawyer, so get your foot off my door."

My foot stayed. "I'm a private cop," I said, "a P.I. looking into Anita's death. If you're innocent, seems to me you'd want to cooperate."

"What you mean, innocent? She killed herself. It's like I told the cops. I knocked, she didn't answer, the door was unlocked, so I went in. I wanted my jacket. If I hadn't had to piss, too, I never woulda found her."

"So you just cut out and left her there?"

"Hell no, my fingerprints were all over her place anyway."

"Yours are on file?" I made it sound half like a question and half like I knew he had a record.

"So what if they are," he said. "All minor stuff. Possession. A couple checks that kited around until they lost their wind." He shrugged away any criminal intent and added, "Look, if she didn't commit suicide—which she did—then I sure as hell didn't kill her."

"Was there any reason for her to commit suicide?"

His face turned into a smirk. "I'd just told her it was over between us. She wasn't a happy camper."

"Think you're a ladies man, huh?"

His face had more of a smirk than a smile. "I have my days . . . and my ways," he said.

I ignored the audacity of his statement. "Was she into pills? She usually take something to get to sleep?"

He shook his head. "No. She didn't even take aspirin. Said she wouldn't adulterate her body." His head jerked as he remembered something else. "Hell, she was a damn vegetarian! It's one of the reasons we broke up. When I get invited to dinner, I want meat and potatoes, not little mouse turds called rice."

"Know anyone who might want her dead?"

He laughed. "Yeah, maybe a cattle rancher or a butcher."

I sighed inwardly. "You sure?"

"Look, man, the only thing I'm sure of is that I got a hot lady in here right now, and I need to get back to her before she cools off, know what I mean? So back your foot up and get outta my face."

I glared, but I moved my foot and watched the door slam shut.

It wasn't a very satisfactory interview. Getting answers out of O'Brien was a real headache. Literally. My head was throbbing. I tromped downstairs to Fisher's Pharmacy for a painkiller and to get a feel for the neighborhood.

I took a box of migraine capsules over to the pharmacist and held it up for him to see. "This stuff really work on heavy-duty pain?" I said. He just shrugged.

I rubbed my temple. "Got anything stronger?"

He smiled. "Sure, with a doctor's prescription."

If I hadn't caught the wary look hiding behind his smile, I wouldn't have pushed it. "Come on," I said, "O'Brien tells me you're a player."

The smile immediately turned sour, and he said, "You can't believe anything an addict says."

Bingo!

I try to keep a twenty waiting in my back pocket for just such an occasion. I threw it on the counter as I read the nametag pinned to the front of his smock. "Look, Fisher, by the time I wait for some doctor to charge his celebrity fee and get back here with the proper paperwork, we'll both be a lot older and I'll still hurt. How 'bout we cut out the middleman and you give me just one little pill?"

He stepped back behind the window of his lab, but not before the twenty disappeared into his pocket. When he came out he slid a small packet at me and murmured, "One time," to tell me I wasn't to come back. With a half salute of thanks, I got the hell out of there.

Outside I checked the packet. A white powder rested in a clear capsule. There was no way on God's earth I was going to take that cap, but I carefully saved it, along with the packet. You never know what might be evidence down the road. Meanwhile, I dry swallowed the migraine pill.

I drove back to my own neighborhood for a beer and a microwaved ham-and-cheese at Frank's bar. Beer can either cause or cure a headache.

It was one of those rare days when Frank opened himself up a little, doing more than looking sympathetic and muttering soothing noises. This time he listened to my list of unanswered questions about Anita's death. When I described Kevin O'Brien he said, "I gotta tell you, Jake, he doesn't sound like the type to fool around with."

"Goes with the territory," I said.

A wag of his head told me he thought I might be wandering where only fools go. There wasn't anything I could say. After that he wrote my tab in his account book without my asking. No wonder Frank's bar is my favorite place away from home.

Melted cheese from the sandwich at Frank's place had taken up squatter's right on my shirt, so I headed back to the office for a clean one. Loretta's car was parked outside. Cora

Lee jumped out the moment she saw me. "Jake!" she yelled. Loretta climbed out of the car and exchanged smiles with me as Cora Lee wrapped herself around my leg   I smiled at her in spite of myself.

I looked at Loretta and said, "What's up?"

"Cora Lee wanted to see you. Says she has something to tell you that no one else can hear, not even me." She started to climb back into the car. "I'll go have coffee with Donna and be back in a few minutes." With that she drove off.

Cora Lee finally let go of my leg, grabbed my hand, and led us to the steps leading into my building. We settled onto a concrete step, and I said, "Okay, what's this all about?"

Somehow she managed to pout and smile at the same time, not saying anything.

"Spit it out," I said.

"Mama's back working at The Hot Cup now that you explained to the guy what happened, but she's looking for a job with more money."

"So?"

"So she needs more sleep than we get in the car. So she'll look good when she goes to see about a different job. *So can we move in with you, Jake*?"

"Now hold on a minute! You know how I live. One room, both office and home. Hardly enough room for myself. Besides, who's going to hire a P.I. with a lady and a scruffy little girl in his office? It wouldn't look right, and it wouldn't *be* right."

"But, Jake . . ."

"Stop right there, Little Miss Missy. I may go along with the unlikely, but I sure as hell am not going to attempt the impossible, and that's what your crazy idea is."

"Mama says nice people don't cuss, Jake."

"So I'm not always a nice person." She just looked at me until I sighed and said, "Okay, kid, I'm sorry. But don't push me, see? I know the car isn't ideal, but you just can't move in with me." The pout on her face was back, so I added, "I'll ask around, okay? Maybe someone will have a cheap room you can call your own."

That did it. She grabbed me in a hug and planted a wet one on my face.

"Don't do that!" I said. "People are going to get the wrong idea. We're right out here in the open." I looked around to be sure no one was watching. "It isn't proper," I said, "so don't do that again."

Believe it or not, she smirked at me. It was either a promise or a threat, I'm not sure which. I just said, "Come on, let's start walking. We'll meet your Mama half way."

Once Cora and her mom were on their way to wherever, I got a fresh shirt and headed for Anita's last place of employment at a retirement home.

The extended-care home was about two blocks from a medical complex and one block from a strip mall that included an optometrist, a Baskin and Robbins, and a medical supply store, everything to be desired by fading eyes, a sweet tooth, and weakened limbs at a retirement home.

It was a sturdy brick building called Caring Arms, a name one notch up from Shady Pines or Twilight Meadows. Anita had been the receptionist. The lobby was utilitarian and shabby. If the resident rooms were this Spartan, the "care" in Caring Arms was overstated and depressing.

However, the present receptionist was sensuous enough to play havoc with any male patient's pacemaker. When I asked for the manager, she smiled at me with pouty lips and said, "Ms. Perkins is in the middle of a conference call right now. If you'll have a seat, it should only be a few minutes."

I sat where I could jump-start my own libido watching her work, craning my neck whenever a slow-moving walker blocked my view. I was startled out of my daydreams when the chair next to me whooshed. Gray hair, wrinkles, polyester, and tight beauty parlor curls had just lowered herself into the plastic chair cushion next to me. "You look like just my type, sonny," Ms. Gray Hair said. The half smile on her face told me she wasn't serious, and I felt strangely disappointed.

"And you look like the type who's too hot for me to handle," I said.

Appreciation straightened her spine as she rested a hand on my arm and learned in close. "That would have been true in my youth," she said. Waving a hand in the direction of the reception desk, she added, "I could have easily outclassed Little Miss Fluffy over there."

I held out my hand. "I don't think you've lost it yet, Mrs. . . ."

"Ketcham. Gertrude Ketcham. But you can call me by my first name."

"And I'm Jake."

I told her I was thinking of getting my grandmother into a retirement home. "I was told I should talk to Anita Brigham," I said, "because she really knows what goes on around here."

An impish look took over her face. "Not much goes on around here. By the time any of us wheel ourselves to where the fun might be, it's already over." The look turned reflective. "But Anita's gone, and they tell us she won't be back. She was such a dear, not like that thing who took her place." Fluffy got another wave of Gertrude's hand.

"What *is* this place like?" I said.

"Don't let the name fool you, Jake. It's a warehouse for throwaway people with money. All they care about is getting our monthly fees on time. The service is lousy and the food not much better." She leaned in closer and whispered, "Anita told me our money wasn't being spent like government regulations dictate." Her head bobbed, waiting for me to take that in before she said, "She told me she was looking into it. Said they'd have to make some changes if they didn't want to lose their license."

I tried to control my eyebrows, but I felt them lift up against my will. As I was about to ask for particulars, Fluffy called out, "Ms. Perkins will see you now."

Poor timing. I was brimming over with questions for Gertrude. I turned and told her I'd be right back, as I started across the lobby.

Several of the smocked workers passing through stared at us as Gertrude grabbed my arm and said, "Any time, Jake. I have a lot more to tell you."

I felt a surge of puppy love as I watched Gertrude settling back into her chair.

Fluffy ushered me into Ms. Perkins' office where I introduced myself. Then her phone rang. With an apologetic look she answered the call and looked up at me as she listened. "Yes, do it right away," she said, before she hung up and waved me into the chair on the other side of her desk.

She wore a business suit that flaunted financial success and a plastic smile that displayed social failure. She raised the hair on the back of my neck, reminding me of a killer spider.

I gave her a spiel about my granny needing professional care, and then I listened to her canned spiel about Caring Arms. She baited her hook with a glowing picture of concern that didn't jibe with the surroundings I'd seen so far. "Just think," she said, "every resident has a roommate to talk to, someone to be a buddy with. And they just have a grand time talking with all the other residents at meals in the dining room. No one is lonely." She turned up the wattage in her smile as she leaned across the desk and added, "They're such cute little things, aren't they?"

Things? Things! I wanted to throw up. Fluffy may be a "cute little thing," but the residents I'd seen were hard put to make the best of what life was dealing late in the game. Cute? Not a chance. Heroic, maybe.

Ms. Plastic carefully steered away from specific costs until after I let my body English tell her I'd swallowed the hook. The monthly payment, she told me, included a shared room, meals, laundry, and dispensing medicine. When I nodded my head like the services were reasonable, she slipped in the actual monthly fee.

Words took over what my brain couldn't accept. "How much?" I blurted.

She knew I'd heard her the first time. "It takes a lot of money to help these dears in their twilight years. You want your grandmother to be happy and comfortable, don't you, Mr. Whittaker?"

My granny would have sold her cookies door to door before she'd move in with these vultures.

I hoped my smile leaned toward compliance. "Is it all right if I talk to some of the staff and residents before I make a decision?"

"Of course. It's our job to help in any way we can. I know your grandmother will be happy and well cared for at Caring Arms."

She dripped sweetness. If I'd been diabetic, I'd have been in a coma.

We shook hands before I left her office. I was wiping her touch off on my pants when I stepped back into the lobby, looking for Gertrude Ketcham.

She was gone.

I stopped one of the smocks and asked about her.

"You a relative?" she said.

"A nephew. Just came in from Chicago to see her."

"We had to take her back to her room. She was very tired."

"She seemed very awake a few minutes ago. She was fine."

She shrugged. "It happens like that sometimes," she said. "And once Gertrude goes to sleep, there's no waking her." She pointed down a hallway and gave me a room number. "You'll see," she said.

Sure enough, Gertrude Ketcham wouldn't have recognized the tooth fairy if he'd crawled from under her pillow. She was comatose and didn't wake up when I called her name or shook her shoulder. I couldn't do anything but pat her hand and whisper that I'd be back.

On my way back to the lobby I could see into most resident rooms, but there was little activity. Tired, bored bodies were either sleeping or staring off into space. I was trying not to believe my own thoughts when a rabbit-looking woman in a smock and a nameplate saying "Nurse Peterson" came out of a room and bumped into me. I could almost see her whiskers twitch. "Oops, sorry," she said, as she clutched a tray with a hypodermic needle and a vial of clear liquid.

"My fault," I said. Then I pointed toward the administrative office. "I was told you could answer some of my questions about Caring Arms. For my grandmother." She looked uncertain. "Are you the one who will be giving my grandmother her medicines?"

She placed her hand over the tray before she spoke. "I dispense doctor's orders, yes. Nothing more."

Woo wee! That was more information than I'd asked for.

"Of course," I said, "but how will my grandmother get her pills from the drug store if she can't walk?"

She visually relaxed. "No problem," she said. "The doctor calls Fisher's Pharmacy, and they deliver to us."

My mind dredged up a window full of designer condoms. "Fisher's on Fifth?" I asked.

"That's right."

My stomach churned, and questions flooded my mind. Was Fisher so greedy that he'd supply pills to an administration that drugged residents to cut expenses? Less activity means less personnel. More drugs means more control. What else was going on at Caring Arms?

A sick depression seeped into my nerve endings. Tomorrow I'd come back to try again with Gertrude Ketcham, but right then I had to get out of there.

The carbon monoxide from traffic outside the building was like a breath of sunshine. I sucked it into my lungs and leaded for my rusty sedan. Even the grimy fast food wrappers littering the back seat smelled better than the hopelessness of Caring Arms.

★★★

Lieutenant Cockran hardly listened to my tale about the possibility of Anita's death being murder. Opening a file, in a bored voice he relayed the facts of the case, pretty much as Mrs. Jameson had told me, then snapped the folder shut. "And so," he said, "the case is closed. Suicide, pure and simple."

"You don't find it too much of a coincidence that Anita might have been about to blow the cover off Caring Arms?"

"So her aunt says, but that charge is completely foundless. Since the day they opened, Caring Arms has come away with only a couple of minor infractions in every state inspection."

"And the boyfriend on drugs? Or the pharmacist who might just like money more than regulations? Don't you think they deserve a little more of a follow up?"

He didn't care. "Be my guest," he said. "I've got too full a caseload to chase rainbows. Your little friend Anita was a young girl who couldn't take rejection. Believe it, and let it be."

I no longer wanted to acknowledge his existence, so I got up, turned my back, and walked away. I had just become a believer. Anita had been murdered, and all I wanted to do was find a killer I could shove down Lieutenant Cockran's throat.

Back outside, I headed for The Hot Cup where I might get my psyche revitalized. It would be good to see Donna and Loretta again, too. And maybe even Cora Lee, though I wasn't admitting that.

★★★

My spirits jumped a notch when I saw Loretta slinging plates at customers. She stopped long enough to thank me again for helping to get her job back. Billy, who had controlled her with the idea that he'd taken Cora Lee, had been put away with a litany of offences, and she and Cora Lee were safe again, except of course that they were still sleeping in the car.

Loretta nodded her head toward Cora Lee sitting behind a coloring book at the far end of the counter.

"Hi, Jake," Cora Lee said when I sat down beside her. Loretta silently brought me a cup of coffee. Cora Lee started to hug me but backed off when I scowled at her and said, "I told you don't do that." I could tell she was a little hurt, but what the hell, she's only a kid.

"Mama's saving to buy a hotplate and a little refrigerator," she said. "We'll need them when you find us a room of our own."

Damn! "Hey, I didn't say I'd *find* a place. I said I'd ask around."

"You'll find us someplace, Jake. It's the kind of thing you do, finding things."

All I could do was shake my head. How in the world did I get messed up listening to a snotty-nosed kid who didn't mean jack shit to me? Instead of having to tell her I probably wouldn't even ask around about a room, I said, "Hey, you want a donut?"

She accepted, of course.

When we finished downing two-day's quota of sugar, she handed me a red crayon and pointed to one of her coloring books. Shit, I don't color cartoon pictures; I can't even stay within the lines of society. Little kid stuff is beyond me . . . but I tried.

When I finally threw the crayon down, she said, "Who are you helping now?"

"A woman who thinks some bad people hurt her niece."

She nodded like she understood. "You'll fix it, Jake. I know you will." Her smile was full of confidence I didn't feel, but when I left there, I was no longer depressed.

★★★

The next morning I woke up ready to do battle. By the time I left Donut Land and headed back to Caring Arms, I was Jake Whittaker, All American P.I.

It was easy slipping into Gertrude's room without being seen. Security seemed to be non-existent at Caring Arms. Her roommate was propped up in bed studying the wall, but Gertrude's bed covers were flat and empty.

"Where's Gertrude?"

"Gone," the weak voice said.

"Gone where?"

"Hospital." She didn't even look at me.

"Which one?"

This time I got no answer. I moved over to her bed and asked a couple more times, but she'd tuned me out.

Damn, was Gertrude all right? Had they overdosed her? Was it because they overheard her talking to me? I had to know she was all right. I headed for a side door and went down the street. I didn't stop until I got to a pay phone. I hit the right hospital on my second call and sped off, pretending octagon signs simply ordered "hesitate."

"Mrs. Ketcham is in intensive care," the pink lady said. "She can't have any visitors."

I love it when I get the information I need without asking—and when I'm handed a challenge like that.

"I'm her priest," I said.

She took in my shiny pants and opened-neck shirt. Pointing to the center of her own neck, she said, "Don't priests wear . . . ?"

"It's optional in my parish."

"Oh." But she wasn't quite sure. "Where's your missal?"

I tapped my head. "Got it all right up here."

"Oh," she said again. She didn't even ask me for identification. Then she handed me a plastic badge that said

"Clergy," pointed to the book on her desk, and said, "Sign in please."

I signed in, reminding myself that I was now Father McFarland from the Church of the Holy Sinners. It had a nice ring to it.

The clergy badge got me accepted at the nurse's station where I asked about Gertrude's condition. Ms. White Cap looked at a file on her desk and said, "The doctor has the test results, but they aren't in her file yet. We think it's her heart."

"Will she be okay? Does she have a history of heart trouble?"

"You'll have to ask her doctor."

"Can I see her now?"

The nurse got up and led me to one of the glass-windowed rooms surrounding the nursing station. "Just five minutes," she said, as she pulled the door shut behind me.

Gertrude looked like a small child sleeping in a huge bed. One tube led up into her nose and another poked through adhesive on the back of her hand. Machines whooshed softly and irregular squiggles on a screen mimicked the rhythm of her heart. I have always hated hospitals, but I hated disease and death more. Gertrude looked like she needed a real priest.

I stood beside her and slipped my hand over hers. I wanted to ask if this was somehow my fault. I wanted to will her to get well so I could help her find a better care facility than Caring Arms.

I wanted revenge for the suffering I imagined was thrust upon her. "Gertrude . . .?" I whispered.

Her eyes didn't open, but a small voice said, "That you, Jake? How'd you get in here?"

She couldn't see my smile. "Today I'm a priest," I said. "Yesterday I was—and really am—a private eye looking into Anita's death."

Her eyes popped open. "Anita's dead?"

Oops. "Yeah, but they say it was suicide."

She seemed to suck in a breath she didn't even have. "Anita wouldn't kill herself!"

"Gertrude, they aren't going to let me stay here much longer, and I have to know some things. Yesterday, before you got sick, did they give you any new pills, something you'd never taken before?"

"Only a vitamin. It wasn't very big."

"And afterwards . . . ?"

"My heart started racing. You don't suppose . . ."

I surrounded her frail hand with both of mine. "I'm gonna find out, I promise you that."

The door opened. White Cap's head poked inside and said, "Time's up."

"I just need a couple of minutes more," I said.

"No, you have to leave right now."

I put professionalism into my voice for White Cap's benefit and said, "I'll be back, Mrs. Ketcham. We still have more prayers to do."

An impish smile managed to appear on Gertrude's face. "No last rites for me, Father. The doctor says I'm going to get better."

★★★

I spent the next three days looking for information about Caring Arms. A friendly face at the city library showed me the index that got me the right reels to feed into the machine. When that proved to be a little past my keen, another efficiency machine on two legs sat me in front of a computer and clicked buttons to get me to where I needed to go. Why didn't they do that in the first place?

What I read raised my eyebrows more than once. My pocket notebook was fatter by several pages when I left there and headed to county and state offices in the same building.

It took two tens to get me the information I needed. I doubt if Lieutenant Cockran had ever run a check on Caring Arms or even checked into the inspection reports on the place. I found stuff that would freak out Stephen King. It sure left me depressed.

It was almost mid-day when I went back to Caring Arms. I tried bypassing Fluffy at the reception desk, but she beat me to Ms. Perkins' door and stood in front of it with her arms out. It was a nice display of feminine charms for me to appreciate. "Oh no you don't," she said. "I'm not about to get fired for letting you go in there without permission." She pointed to one of the chairs I'd sat in the day before. "You'll have to wait."

I had several choices. Roughing up Fluffy would definitely be against my mother's training. Yelling at Perkins through the door would be rather uncouth, though I wasn't sure why I should care. And sitting down and waiting would be frustrating but prudent. I chose option three. I reminded Fluffy of my name, and sat down.

Ten minutes later I was granted an audience with Ms. Perkins, the esteemed ruler of Caring Arms. Ms. Plastic Perkins sat with an open ledger, feeding numbers into a calculator. I got a fake welcome and a motion to sit down.

When she finally looked up, she said, "Good morning, Mr. Whittaker. Have you made a decision about your grandmother?"

"What I need is answers to a lot of questions."

Her smiled remained in place. "Of course. We want your loved one to be fully taken care of."

I wanted to gag. "Like you take care of those other poor souls out there?" My voice showed all the sarcasm I felt.

"I beg your pardon?"

I leaned across the desk to get my face into hers. "I'm talking about Gertrude Ketcham conveniently landing in the hospital yesterday after I talked to her. I'm talking about residents being given drugs that doctors didn't prescribe."

She sputtered in her answer. "I . . . we never . . . we always . . ."

I couldn't hold still for the deceit and the lies. I jumped to my feet so fast she rebounded into the back of her chair without my even touching her. "Do you really think your nurses will lie under oath?" I spat at her.

The color drained from her face, and she said, "We have nothing to hide."

I pulled out my pocket notebook and read a few lines to her, quotes from different agencies' reports after inspecting Caring Arms. I ended up with the one that said, "This agency believes the residents may be unnecessarily medicated."

With that she blew it. There were no more pretenses as she blurted out, "I'd like to see them try doing this job! All we want to do is make things more manageable here."

"They're *people*, not *things*!"

I stood there and stared at her. It was quiet for a moment as I began to pace the floor and she tried to make amends by saying, "I didn't mean it that way."

I turned to face her. "Did you mean it when you gave Gertrude a so-called vitamin yesterday?"

This time she sat up tall. "It *was* a vitamin. Gertrude had an unexpected heart seizure yesterday. It had nothing to do with any prescription pills."

There was still fear and uncertainty in her voice, but I let that pass for the moment. Leaning on the desk, I said, "What about the barbiturates that killed Anita?"

Her head jerked with the word "killed." "My God," she said, "I . . . we didn't do anything to Anita. *Whatever she took didn't come from here.*"

The statement told me a lot. Perkins was still thinking Anita's death was a suicide, that she took the pills herself. Maybe she and her white-capped cronies hadn't killed Anita to save themselves. "Maybe" would have to do until I covered all bets and was looking at the winning hand. Meanwhile I just stared at Perkins.

Her spine compressed, and all confidence oozed out of her. "What do you want from me, Mr. Whittaker?"

I sat back down and starting telling her how the world was going to evolve. I mentioned words like "scandal" and "attempted murder." She took on the look of a cornered mouse too scared to fight.

I don't remember what my parting words were. I only remember how dirty I felt inside and out as the door to Caring Arms closed behind me. At a time like that there was only one thing to do. I headed for Frank's bar where I could do battle again with my old foes Anger and Frustration. My first beer went down with silence, but I needed diversion with the second one. "Gimme the phone," I called out to Frank.

It took four rings before Mrs. Jameson answered. My voice told her my mood. "No progress?" she said.

"Oh yeah. I opened a can and a whole mess of worms came creeping out. Anita knew more than was good for her."

I heard the squeak of her wheelchair wheels before she answered. "Do you think she was murdered?"

"Oh yeah. My call is that she was about to become an upright citizen who didn't like exploitation, and someone got scared of the fallout. Also, I'm sorry to say, she had a lousy choice in a boyfriend."

"I already told you that. As the kids say, he was a total creep."

"There seems to be nothing *but* creeps on this case."

"Which creep do you think killed Anita?"

"I don't know yet, but I plan to find out."

After a few more words, we hung up and I ordered lunch while I nursed the second beer. It was clearing up outside when I left about an hour later.

★★★

O'Brien was coming out of a drug fog when I arrived at his walkup over Fisher's Pharmacy. When he finally answered my insistent knocking, he looked like hell. His face was pasty and pale, his eyes couldn't focus, and his hair looked like a fright wig on Halloween. He'd bottomed out. His brain recognized me, though. "I haven't got time, man," he said. "It was a bad night."

"So I see." I shouldered my way in before he could rally his muscles to block me. The chaos of his place made my office look like *House Beautiful.* "Sit," I commanded. "I'm going to ask questions, and you're going to answer them. You hold back or lie to me and I'll find your stash and destroy it." He was in no condition to resist, and I hoped he was in no condition to think of plausible lies.

He sat on an empty pizza box in a chair. I cleared the coffee table with one sweep of my hand and sat on it, facing him. The debris hitting the floor seemed to bring him out of his fog, but he tried to look belligerent instead of just wiped out or scared. I wasn't in the mood to sort out his feelings. I wanted words. "What did Anita tell you about Caring Arms?" I said. "The truth."

He looked at my face before answering. "They weren't going by state regulations."

"What else?"

His voice got very little. "Drugs."

"What about drugs?"

"They were drugging the old fogies, okay?"

"How did she know?"

"I don't know. It's what she told me. She said too many of them were 'out of it.'"

"Where'd they get the drugs?"

"How the hell should I know?"

By this time my elbows were leaning on my knees, and my face was pushing him into the back of his chair. "Where do you get yours?" I demanded.

He shrugged and said, "Here. There."

A light bulb went off in my head. "Cut the crap. Fisher's downstairs is your only supplier, isn't he?"

The voice got small again. "So what?" he said.

"I think Anita was going to blow the whistle on Caring Arms and your supplier was gonna get caught in the crossfire."

"Fisher told me it was all gonna be cool."

"You told Fisher about what Anita thought?" He shrugged again, admitting he had. Holy shit! I got to my feet to give my brain more room to think. The pieces began to fall in place. Now all I needed was to pull a rabbit out of a hat.

I left O'Brien to further abuse his body and walked slowly back to my car, wanting to get all the ducks in my mind lined up before I went any further. I took a stale Milky Way out of the glove box, hoping the sugar rush would pull me through the next hour.

My ducks were quacking in unison as I walked back to Fisher's Pharmacy. He took one look at my face and headed for the windowed sanctuary of his pharmacy lab. I had no qualms about following right behind him.

When he saw me behind him, he started to reach for a switch marked "talk" near a computer screen, but I wasn't about to let him get rid of me by broadcasting I was trespassing over any intercom. I knocked his hand away and let him see the switch was off limits. "This is a private talk," I said. "The name's Whittaker, and a sweet old lady almost died because of you!"

"What the hell are you talking about?"

Why does everyone with a guilty secret always say that?

"Caring Arms is what I'm talking about. No doctor prescribed whatever was given to Gertrude Ketcham to keep her from talking to me."

His face showed the beginning of fear. "Ketcham?" he said, walking past me to the computer. He punched at keys and stared at the screen before saying, "I've never had a prescription for a Ketcham."

"Of course not. You supply without prescriptions, just like you do for Kevin upstairs, just like you did for me yesterday."

He was still staring at the computer, a machine way out of my league. Shoot, I don't even have a cell phone, because who in the world would I call anyway?

Fisher's fingers left the computer keys. He turned to look at me like I was a bug that needed squashing. "You needed help," he said. "I took pity on you and gave you one pill."

"Is that the excuse you tell yourself? I'm not sure that's the way others, like the Pharmacy Board, will see it." I figured there had to be some such agency.

His face took on the look of a fighter who had just taken a hard punch, but he turned back to the computer. I hardly understand my Olivetti typewriter, so I was amazed as his fingers flew across the keys. It was only when I saw the word "delete" show up in a little window that I jumped in and knocked his hands away, putting myself between Fisher and the computer. "What the hell were you deleting?" I yelled.

A wicked smile appeared on his face. "My drug ordering and inventory program seems to have developed a glitch," he said. "And phone orders don't have signatures." He leaned back against the opposite wall, full of himself.

He no longer looked worried about the computer, but I stayed between him and the keyboard. He gave me a Cheshire Cat look, crossed his arms, and wagged his head in satisfaction. That's when I remembered some of the parting words I'd given to Ms. Perkins at Caring Arms. Along with "attempted murder," I mentioned "accessory" and finished my litany with "murder one." I laid it all out to Fisher with the same accusing words.

Like a deflating balloon, his arms fell to his sides as he slumped sideways against some metal shelving. "I didn't . . ."

My elbows jammed backwards as though punctuating my words. "You did," I said. "First you fattened your pockets through the misery of old people and miserable addicts like Kevin. Then you killed Anita because she was about to blow the lid off Caring Arms."'

He straightened up. "It's my word against theirs. Besides, I had no motive to kill Anita."

"But you did, didn't you? You were afraid for your pharmaceutical license." I kept my eyes on his until he was forced to look down.

After a moment he snorted, and he looked up and stared at me. "She made the mistake of coming in here and telling me she thought Perkins was giving me fake prescriptions. The little bitch said she was going to the police and wanted me to back her up against Perkins." His anger at Anita showed in his words. "She also made the mistake of telling me she had a bad cold," he said. This time he gave a small laugh. "I mixed up a potent vitamin C capsule for her. Told her not to take it before she got home 'cause it might make her sleepy."

I wanted to hear him say it. "And so you killed her?"

"I gave her a capsule, that's all."

"And you were just going to let her go to the police? You weren't afraid for your own skin? You had to know Perkins would roll over on you when the chips were down."

"Her word against mine."

"Nurses know more than you think they know. You think the nurses are going to back either you or Perkins?"

The air seemed to go out of him. He stood there with his eyes not really seeing anything.

"And so you killed her," I said again.

His fight was gone. He said, "Yeah, I killed her, but I'll never say that to anyone else. It's my word against yours, Whittaker." He tried to smile but couldn't quite make it.

Then it was my turn to smile. "It's your own words that will convict you, Fisher," I said. I pulled away from the counter I had been leaning on and pointed at the switch marked "talk" beside the computer. When he saw the intercom was open, his face turned ashen. He hadn't known how talented I can be with my elbows.

Fisher turned to look through the glass window at the pharmacy store beyond his lab. Customers and employees stood stock still, staring at us through the window. They had heard his confession, loud and clear. My feet wanted to do a little River Dance jig right there in one place, but there was no way I could keep my arms still. Instead I mimicked a phone at my ear, signaling someone to make a call to the police. Then I planted myself between Fisher and the door.

We waited. It felt good.

When the siren sound got close I relaxed a little, but Fisher was already a puddle of putty. It took a while for the uniforms to sort out the constant jabbering of customers and employees, but by the time Lieutenant Cockran arrived I felt really great. "I told you Anita was murdered," I told him. I straightened my spine to my full five-feet-ten-inches, pointed at Fisher, and said, "And there's the perp." Cockran's sneer rolled right off me.

★★★

When I left the precinct several hours later, it was raining again, but it felt like sunshine to me. I'd earned my per diem with stars and fireworks. A little inner voice told me Gertrude would soon make it out of intensive care and that visiting in a hospital wasn't so bad after all. I'd make sure she moved into a place *waay* above Caring Arms. Maybe she even knew how to play gin rummy and could give me a run for my money. Maybe I'd bring Cora Lee with me.

CHAPTER 3
FOR THE BIRDS

Cora Lee was in my office for a couple of hours while Loretta hunted for a better-paying job. It wasn't my choice. Loretta had smiled at me, and Cora Lee had smiled at me. I felt sour at the suggestion that I baby-sit, but somehow their smiles won. Cora Lee was reading a book about pioneers traveling across country with the family cow, and I was writing a little fiction in a client report. My mind was as cluttered as my desk when the office door opened and a heavenly vision walked in. Childhood smiles, books, and reports flew from my mind.

My ears heard her whisper, "Mr. Whittaker?" but it was my eyes that registered her presence. She was gorgeous. She had curves in all the right places. And she also had a face that couldn't decide if it wanted to be angelic or devilish. My imagination shifted into high gear. Good golly, how could I be having such thoughts with an eight-year-old in the room! "Um, Cora Lee," I said. "Do you suppose you could visit Mrs. Clement down the hall while I talk to this nice lady?"

"I'll just sit here and read, Jake," she said. "I won't say a word."

Ms. Vision smiled at me, and then she smiled at Cora Lee. Damn, she was going to think Cora Lee was mine. "No!" I said to Cora Lee, perhaps a little too emphatically. "Mrs. Clement can take over the baby sitting for a little while. Go on, I won't be long."

Cora Lee didn't say anything, but I heard her shuffle from the room. I didn't see the office door shut, but then my eyes were elsewhere. I cleared my throat and realized how my office must look to someone who obviously had everything in exactly the place it should be. At least I had folded the blanket at the end of the fake-leather couch that also serves as my bed. The file cabinet with the cans of chili on top was dinged up, but it was green and cheerful.

But then there was me, wearing the same clothes as yesterday, struggling to look professional with a client I desperately wanted to impress. What could I do but smile sheepishly and explain, "Baby-sitting for a friend." Then I pointed to the ratty chair across the desk and somehow managed to add, "Call me Jake."

She gave me a 1000-watt smile, settled her lovely hips into the chair, and crossed her perfect legs. I tried not to stare. "My name is Melissa Allgood," she said.

I hoped the surname was a male rating rather than a moral creed.

I sighed and tried to remember I'm a professional who could use a new client. "What can I do for you, *Ms.* Allgood?"

"Miss," she corrected, reading some of my thoughts. If she had read all of them, she would have slapped my face. "My friend Georgina told me you might be able to help me, Mr. Whittaker."

"Jake," I reminded her as I grabbed a pencil and fished into the wastebasket for an unpaid bill to write on.

"And you can call me Melissa."

I smiled. "If you're looking for an excellent private investigator, Melissa, I'm sure I can help you." I told her my per diem and said expenses were extra.

"Money's no problem," she said. That did it; now I totally adored her.

"So, Melissa, how can I help?"

"Patty has been missing for two days."

"Who's Patty? Your daughter?"

"No, she's my bird."

The point of my pencil snapped. "Excuse me, Love, I'm a P.I., not the Humane Society. Birds have wings..."

"But Patty couldn't—wouldn't—have flown off." The 1000-watt smile was back. "You have to help me find her, Jake."

We both knew I couldn't—wouldn't—turn her down. "What happened?" I said.

"I came home Wednesday and found her cage open." Tears formed in corners of her eyes. "She's nowhere in the house. Someone has to have taken her."

I cleared my throat. My next question was standard for a missing person, but in this case it sounded foolish. "Would the bird... would Patty... have any reason to fly off?"

"Of course not! We're friends. She loves eating pears with me. We're so close she even takes bites right off my lips."

As I watched her lips say those words, goose bumps rose on my arms. First time I ever considered being a bird. I cleared my throat again. "So, okay, is there anyone who has a reason to harm Patty, or steal her?"

"Well, Jake, Mrs. Wilson next door doesn't like me, although I don't know why because I get along fine with Mr. Wilson. But the Mrs. sure grabs the fruit that drops off my tree into her yard!"

"Fruit?"

"My pear tree." She grinned at me and added, "After all, a girl has to eat right to keep her figure, doesn't she?"

I wasn't about to dispute her success with that. "Anyone else?"

"Not unless you count Johnny Galetti."

"From *the* Galetti family?"

"Yeah, but Johnny owns a legitimate restaurant. You know, 'Exotic-Erotic." Yeah, I knew about it. Exotic game served by erotic topless waitresses. "Real upscale," she added.

I tried not to grin. I knew the place but had never been there. "So, what's Johnny's problem?" I said.

"He stomped off because I got up to feed Patty in the middle of . . . well, I thought he'd fallen asleep, and Patty needs to be fed on time, you know."

"That's it? He left mad because you fed your bird?"

"Yeah."

"You got a picture of Patty?"

She reached into a purse hugging one lip and handed me a snapshot. I expected a canary or even a parrot, but Patty was a fat little thing with stripes on her breast and a Lone Ranger mask across her eyes and down into her neck. If Johnny's restaurant was into serving quail, Patty would have made a tasty side dish.

She held out a small card. "Here's my address so you can check out the neighborhood. You can find Johnny at his restaurant."

I nodded as though I might actually consider trying to find her bird, but I was searching for the right words to tell her it was hopeless when she stood up and smoothed down her skirt by running red-tipped fingers down her hips. That did it. My mouth wouldn't open, and words of refusal wouldn't come. I didn't even dare to have her see me if I stood up.

She reached across the desk to shake my hand. "Can I expect to hear from you tomorrow?" You could toast bread with the electricity that passed between our fingers. Like a ceramic dog in the back window of a car, my head was still bobbing up and down when she sauntered out of my office.

Cora Lee must have been watching in the hallway, because she was back immediately with a smirk on her face. "You look silly," she said. "I think that lady made you silly." I knew she wasn't going to allow me to ignore her, but I tried. I didn't need a grade school analyst in my life right then. "You gonna find that Patty bird for her, Jake?" she said.

"You were listening?"

"Of course." I tried to think if I'd said anything to Ms. Allgood too adult for sensitive ears. I couldn't remember.

"Will you try to find her bird?" she asked again.

"Yeah, I'll try," I said.

She smiled at me before heading back to her book, but she stopped for a moment, looked back over her shoulder, and said, "It's okay to be silly sometimes, Jake. Silly can be good, my mom says."

I don't know if I felt silly right then, but I do know I felt good.

★★★

Melissa's house was on a busy street in a family section of town where people would have left doors unlocked in earlier years. I parked my ride on the corner and walked the block to get the feel of the neighborhood. People were out enjoying the afternoon sun, away from TV. There was a feeling of security and pride in the houses, a place where you knew the mailman's name and the time of day your neighbors left for work. It was Saturday, a day when the little kids played hopscotch on the sidewalk and the big kids sat on outdoor stairs and knocked their heads together in laughter.

Just as I spotted Melissa's house, a business suit with a small briefcase turned up her front walk. He set the case down, rang the doorbell, waited, and then peeked into the windows when no one answered.

I walked up behind him and said, "Hello," startling the guy so he almost fell off the stoop. I love it when I can do that!

He held his hand to his heart. "You Mr. Allgood?" he said. I shook my head. "Well, regardless, she asked if I had bird magazines in addition to the usual magazines I'm selling. She owes me the balance on the subscriptions I sold her. You know when she'll be back?"

I might have known: a drummer, selling magazines no one wants anyway.

"I'm just a visitor, too," I said. "Guess you'll have to come back when she's home."

"Damn broad," he said. Then he raised his hands to dismiss that and added, "Oh well, Johnny said she's good for it."

"Johnny Galetti?"

"That's right. At the Exotic-Erotic."

"You wouldn't happen to know anything about her bird, would you?"

"What bird? Didn't know she had one." He looked rather disgusted. "And what's her owing me money got to do with a bird anyway?"

"I'll tell you what might have happened," I said. "You could have come back earlier for your money, seen the bird through the window, and thought you'd take it as collateral till Ms. Allgood paid in full." It was far-fetched, but it was just the sort of thing a weasel salesman would do.

My face must have told him what I thought of him, because the little rodent backed off a pace and said, "Hey, I may earn a buck however I can, but I didn't cop no stupid bird." With that he picked up his silly little briefcase, said, "Tell her I'll be back tomorrow." He walked off with a macho arrogance that wasn't half bad.

I got out my pocket notebook and put the drummer down as a suspect. He was money-hungry without much compassion. Hell, maybe he took Melissa's Patty to sell to Galetti for his restaurant. I hate salesmen.

★★★

A couple doors down a panel truck with the words "Peterson's Piping" was parked beside a man leaning over an open trench with the crack of his ass staring up at me. I leaned down and said, "Whatcha doin'?"

He stopped working long enough to say, "Trying for two days to find a damn water leak. That is, when I don't have to stop for stupid questions."

I pointed to Melissa's house. "A pet bird was lost over there a couple of days ago. I wonder if you saw anyone suspicious."

"Like you, you mean?"

I managed to smile. "Yeah, like me—but not so good lookin'."

"What kind of bird? One of them silly canaries?"

"No, a quail."

"Oh, a bobwhite."

"No, a quail."

"Bobwhite, quail. Same bird, different names. And no, I ain't seen no *quail*."

I thanked him and turned to walk away. "*Tweet, tweet,*" he called out after me.

Just for that I got out my notebook and added him to my suspect list. A wise-ass plumber is just as nefarious as a drummer.

As I finished writing, a loud cheer went up behind a house across the street, so I crossed over at the end of the block and headed down the alley. The cheering came from one yard filled with a huge skateboard ramp made of several pieces of plywood forced into a rounded U-shape. Standing around the ramp was a bunch of teenage lords, thugs in tight-fitting shirts, jeans, and knee pads. My loose gabardines and Hawaiian shirt felt out of place.

Another cheer rose up as the boy on the ramp scooted to the very top of one high end, did a one-eighty leap, and headed back down again. The kid was good. When he ran out of steam I stepped in and said, "Great moves."

They all turned to look at me. "What's your problem, dude?" one sneering face said.

"Just a couple questions, that's all. I'm a P.I. investigating the disappearance of a pet bird from this neighborhood."

"Ooo, a pet bird!" one of them said. "What's it got to do with us?"

"Maybe you saw something. It happened two days ago at Miss Allgood's."

"Oh, Melissa. Well, we'd do anything to help Melissa, huh guys?" This was greeted with shrill whistles and lusty grunts.

It was time to give these Neanderthals a dose of comeuppance. "Listen, you punks, the lady is *Miss Allgood* to you. Remember that."

It was as though I hadn't said a thing. They were on a roll of their own. "Hey, maybe the bird got out on its own." Smart ass!

"Yeah, maybe it flipped the deadbolt with its little beak and turned the knob with its little feet." Laughter and footstomping filled the air, and they ignored me by turning back to the ramp as one young hood took his turn on the ramp. Wanting my daily report to show all contacts, I made a note about my encounter with these skateboard lords before continuing down the alley.

I heard music pumping from a screened porch, heavy bass notes calling to male hormones. Bump-and-grind, pure burlesque music. Like a Peeping Tom, I shaded by eyes from the sun and peered out from behind a board fence at three women in tight, short skirts. They were on a porch, grinding with the music and thrusting a hip with each bump note, laughing every time. My face broke into a smile as I watched them. They may not have had the rhythm of the gals down at the Pussy Cat, but they sure as hell were having more fun.

Questions for these women would have to wait until they wouldn't be caught in the act and be highly embarrassed, so I put the bawdy dancing ladies in my notebook to remind me to question them later, if needed.

With nothing else to see in the alley, I walked back to the front of the houses. An ice cream truck marked "Cool Maids" had showed up, and kids were walking home with ice cream treasures. When everyone else was gone, I stepped up to the truck's serving window and said, "Where you here a couple of days ago?"

"One of us is here every day, all summer," the woman inside said.

"Then you know what goes on in the neighborhood?"

"Look, mister, what I know is ice cream. We women started this business to get away from creeps like you." I blinked, getting far more than my question warranted. "If we see anything, we aren't about to tell the likes of you." She pointed to the words "Cool Maids" on the truck and added, "We serve cool stuff, period."

"Okay, that's cool," I said.

She didn't appreciate my subtle joke. She said, "So what'll you have?"

"How much for an ice cream bar?"

She pointed to a list of items with prices posted on the side of the truck and said, "Two bucks."

"For just one?" The word was half question and half disbelief.

I got a sneer. "Yeah, each one."

I looked at the product list and chose the cheapest item. "Gimme a strawberry pushup then."

"Like it says, they're two for . . ."

"I only want one."

She slapped a red sleeve of paper on the counter and said, "Got a buck, big spender?" I threw a crumpled bill down, snatched up my frozen ice, and took off. I stopped long enough to write a reminder to myself to try again tomorrow. Maybe a different Cool Mail would stop milking customers long enough to answer my questions. Right then I was going to eat my strawberry slush.

When I had licked out the last of the ice, I shoved the deflated cylinder in my pocket, crossed back to Melissa's side the street and worked my way to the alley behind her house.

Two doors down was an in-ground swimming pool in the back yard. An adolescent female punched down on the diving board and flipped up for a perfect swan dive. As she pulled herself out of the pool, I yelled, "Bravo!"

"Listen, mister, don't go getting any ideas."

"Hang on . . ." I fumbled for my wallet and flashed the Junior G-Man badge I once ordered from a cereal box. "Just a couple of questions, that's all."

"I told the other officer all I know."

Other officer? What the hell? I jumped in with both feet and said, "Yeah, right, but I need to hear it for myself." I tried to look needy, saying, "Please."

She told me about her mother's jewelry being stolen two days ago, probably while she had been swimming and practicing her diving. After giving me the details, she hung her head down and said, "You guys gonna get my mom's jewelry back?"

"We're gonna try, Sweetheart." A gut feeling told me the jewel thief could also have let Patty out. Another gut feeling tried to get my attention, but I couldn't quite grab hold of it. I thanked her for telling her story again and took off, stopping only long enough to pull out my notebook and write myself a reminder to talk to the swan diver's parents.

The last house before I hit the sidewalk at the end of the alley had a deck with three teenage blondes in bikinis presenting their bodies to the sun. I stared for a moment or two before calling out, "Excuse me!"

All three heads lifted to look at me, and all three burst out in giggles. No shit, they took one look at me and giggled like a gaggle of geese. Finally one of them said, "What is it, mister?"

"I'm a private eye working for Miss Allgood."

"Well, if Miss Sexy Pants has a problem, we're not about to help her," one of them said, and the others tuned in with another chorus of giggles. In frustration I gave up and made another notebook reminder to talk to the silly geese later, maybe in the presence of their parents.

There were too many reminders in my notebook and not enough real info. I went home feeling like I wasn't earning my keep.

★★★

I cranked open a can of chili and set the can on the hot plate. The coils were doing their thing as I fished clean clothes from a file drawer. Grabbing my soap, razor, and towel bag, I headed down the hall to clean up in the men's room. Feeling somewhat better, I used a spoon to stir the chili and ate it right out of the can, enjoying even the crust of beans at the bottom.

My spirits lifted after I found Melissa's card and dialed her number. "Jake here," I said.

"Jake! Have you found my Patty?"

I took one breath and did the only honest thing I could: I lied. "I'm making some progress," I said. I could sense her disappointment.

"You talk to Johnny yet?"

"Tomorrow."

She was quiet again, punctuated only by a soft sniffling. I offered some soothing words, and we hung up with my promise to be at her house after I'd been to Johnny's place. I had a lot of thinking to do, so I headed for Frank's bar where the pretzel bowls are always full and Frank knows when to shut up. I ordered a beer and motioned at the jar of hard-boiled eggs behind the bar.

"Bad day?" Frank asked as he set an egg on a napkin for me..

"The worst. I have a sexy dream of a client with a nightmare of a case. If I don't get lucky . . . I won't get lucky."

He got my beer, shot me a look of sympathy, and said, "Want to tell me about it?"

I patted the air with my hand to tell him it was too complicated, and he left me to my thoughts.

The wet beer bottle made a golden ring on the counter. I circled it with my finger, tuning out the smoke and noise. My mind clawed at something I'd seen or heard during the day, but I couldn't pull it to the surface.

I seldom have more than a couple of beers, but that day I found myself looking down at five beer bottle circles on the bar, all joined together like an Olympic symbol drawn by a drunk. Perhaps they were. I knew I wouldn't be too steady on my feet when I got up.

Time to go home. But first I drew the five bottle rings in my notebook to remind myself of answers hiding beneath the surface of my questions earlier in the day.

★★★

I slept clear through into the next afternoon and had to use yesterday's coffee to jump-start my body. My head hurt, and my knees felt weak. I knew I wasn't a pretty picture.

Somehow I got dressed and headed for the Exotic-Erotic. They were beginning to set up for dinner, and I had to flash my G-Man badge at the young stuff at the door to get in. "Johnny Galetti?" I barked. He pointed down a hallway at the far end of the dining room.

I took in the atmosphere as I headed that way. The place was disgusting with the stuffed heads of dead animals hanging on the walls. I kept my eyes down until I got to a door marked "Staff Only." The doorknob turned when I tried it, so I walked in. The room had a bank of file cabinets with two beautiful females using phones at separate desks. I could almost smell illegal activities.

The redhead hung up and said, "Who the hell are you?"

I did my G-Man badge shtick, and it worked again.

She smiled and got up to dig her fingers into the shoulder of the other girl. The blonde looked up, saw me, and said, "Call you back." Then she hung up.

"Whittaker," I said. "You the bookkeepers?"

"She's across the hall."

"So what are you? Secretaries?"

The redhead curled a lip and said, "Hardly." She paused long enough to gather a lie and said, "We're the purchasing agents."

"For the exotic animals?"

This time it was the blonde who chimed in with, "Yeah, for them. What's the problem, officer?" Before I could respond she added, "Listen, mister, you have any questions about the restaurant, you should talk to Mr. Galetti.."

I stood and looked at them. "Okay," I said, "I'll do just that." None of us said goodbye as I left the room and shut the door behind me. I added the gorgeous birds to my notebook. Maybe they knew something I needed to know, but mostly it felt good to picture them as I wrote.

Across the hall I knocked at the bookkeeper's door. An older, self-confident woman in a no-nonsense skirt and oversized glasses pulled the door open.

"You the bookkeeper?"

"*Oui*," the accented voice said.

Oh goody, a Mama hen who spoke French. This one looked too savvy to fall for the G-Man badge, so I pulled a bluff instead. "I've been sent to get some answers," I said.

"I will answer your questions, Monsieur—as long as it does not concern Monsieur Galetti's *prive affaires*."

I was saved from thinking up bookkeeper-type questions by the slam of another door. "That Mr. Galetti comin' in?"

"I think he's already in his office."

I fingered a quick salute to her and said, "I'll get back to you."

"*Oui*," she said again, as she closed the door behind me. I quickly added Madame Hen's name to my notebook. There was more going on here than just a restaurant. I could smell it. I smelled money that wasn't earned with just a couple drinks and an exotic steak.

I stood staring at the office door marked "No Admittance." Resigned at having to face Johnny Galetti, I knocked. "Not now!" a gruff voice said.

It was shit-or-get-off-the-pot time, so I barged in anyway. Before anything could register in my brain, I'd slammed the door behind me.

Good golly, Miss Molly, what a sight! Two bodies leaning over the desk, one facing up, one facing down. Skirt up; pants down. Movement was arrested, but legs still stuck out at odd angles. This was truly a pretty sight!

"Who the hell are you?" the guy yelled. He shifted a little to block my view and pulled away from the desk. The woman unraveled herself behind him, stood up, rearranged her clothing, and darted out through a door on the other side of the room.

Galetti was tall and trim enough, but he had one of those thin little beard lines that fell from his ears and burst into a goatee under his chin. Slimy trying to be sophisticated.

"Whittaker," I said. "Jake Whittaker."

His face was red with anger and embarrassment. "And just what part of 'not now' don't you understand, Whittaker?"

"The part that says you're cheating on Miss Allgood."

He stretched himself up tall, forgetting his embarrassment and letting his anger take over. "What business is it of yours?" he said. When I said nothing, he backed down slightly. He waved at the door where the woman had scooted out and shrugged. "Hey, you understand," he said. "It's part of the business. Gotta keep 'em happy." *A definite sleaze ball.*

I went for broke. "So what were you doing at Miss Allgood's place two days ago when she wasn't home?"

"How'd you . . .?" He stopped and watched my face break into a grin. "What the hell," he said, "I was about to break it off anyway."

"Then why break into her place?"

"I gave her some diamond earrings I wanted to pass on to Barbie, but I couldn't find them with her other jewelry."

"So instead you stole her bird to sell as one of your restaurant's exotic birds."

"I don't need to steal no birds. Besides, customers want flamingos or puffins, not some common shit like Melissa's got."

I wasn't buying it. "But you do have a key to her place." His face told me my guess was right. "Yeah, so what?"

"So I think you let yourself in and copped the bird."

He smirked at me and said, "Maybe I did; maybe I didn't."

I started to close up the distance between us. He took it as the threat it was. "Okay, okay," he said. "Take it easy. So I let the damn bird out."

"Out of the cage?"

"Outside. Out of the house."

I exploded. "What the hell for?"

"For spite. The damn thing got more attention than I did."

This time I completely closed up the distance between us and said, "You and Miss Allgood are through all right, as of right now." I leaned into his face and added, "You stay away from her!"

I hoped I looked tough as I swaggered out of the room and slammed the door behind me.

The two turtledoves, Johnny and Barbie, went into my notebook.

★★★

The next day Loretta brought Cora Lee to my office, asking if I could watch her for just that day. I told her no, that I had places I needed o be. "I have a job to do," I told her. "No work; no pay."

My problems went right over her head. "This is a really important interview, Jake," she said. When I still balked, she said, "She can wait in the car for you wherever you go. *Please*, Jake." The next thing I knew, Cora Lee was peering into my face with a sappy, pleading face. But of course the sap was me. As my head bobbed up and down in surrender, I mentally wondered why people couldn't be born at, say, fifteen years old at least. I'd been out manipulated by an eight-year-old.

Cora Lee had her usual pile of books with her and was telling me about one of the stories as I drove to Melissa's place. My mind was on Cora Lee's books when we passed a Barnes and Noble store, and my mind slammed into gear. *Books!* I pictured that salesman peddling his subscriptions down Melissa's street. His briefcase probably held some sample magazines, *and it was large enough to hide stolen jewelry.*

Gotcha! The little weasel was really using spiel of magazine subscriptions to peek inside every house. Then later he could rob them when no one was home. Well, I was about to put a stop to it. I found a working pay phone and called the local burglary division. With the information I gave, it would be easy for them to locate the drummer if he was still working the same area. I wouldn't get paid for helping bring the perp down, but when I got back in my car I felt like a kid who just hit his first home run.

I hate salesmen!

★★★

"You wait here," I told Cora Lee when we got to Melissa's. "I do a solo act." I didn't tell her that I also didn't want her to see me ogling Melissa.

"Please, please let me come with you," she said. "I'll be ever so quiet, honest I will."

She was already cramping my style by just being outside Melissa's house; I wasn't about to let her inside. "No!" I said.

"You lock the doors and stay here. Got that?" She pouted, but she nodded her head as I closed the car door behind me.

"*Jaaake!*" Melissa drawled as she stepped back to let me in. She wore a saucy red dress that hugged her hips and flounced out above the knees. For the first time I was jealous of a piece of fabric.

Then she looked out and saw Cora Lee in the car. "That your little friend again?" she said. When I shrugged, she misunderstood and said, "Yes, of course she's welcome to come in, too." Before I could protest, Melissa motioned to Cora Lee and called out, "Come on in, sweetheart."

Cora Lee's eyes bored into mine, asking permission. What could I do with both Melissa and Cora Lee waiting for me to answer? I motioned Cora Lee to come in. As we followed Melissa into the house, I whispered to Cora Lee, "One word out of you and you're history. Understand?" She nodded her head, but an impish smile also spread across her face. I'd see to her later.

When we were all seated in the living room, Melissa said, "Did you find my Patty?"

I signed, feeling completely defeated. There was nothing I could offer this gorgeous woman who offered so much to anyone with eyes. I pulled out my pocket notebook and tapped it on my knee. "Well," I finally said, "I have all kinds of suspects in here, people I saw and talked to. Some are good possibilities." I tried to sound more hopeful than I felt. She looked expectant, like I was going to magically tie it all together and reunite her with Patty. "The answer's here; I can feel it in my bones . . ." I began again.

"First of all," I said, "Galetti is the one who let Patty out of the house when he came to collect the earrings he had given you."

"So that's where they went!" she said. "Well, I feel betrayed. That's the end of him in my life." I didn't tell her Galetti was already out of her life.

I watched as her face became putty and her eyes started to tear. I wanted to throw my arms around her and never let go. But there was Cora Lee, ready to cry herself. Damn, why did Cora Lee have to be there?

"So my Patty is gone. *Gone.*"

"Don't give up yet," I whispered to Melissa. "Let me show you what I do know." I flipped open the notebook and explained to her the people I'd seen and talked to. By the time I'd run down the list, both Melissa and Cora Lee were leaning toward me, listening, hoping, trying to understand where I was leading them, when I had no idea I was leading anywhere.

We were quiet for a moment or two before Melissa reached for a small framed picture of Patty on the table beside her. She stared at the picture and murmured, "Poor Patty. My poor Patty."

Cora Lee learned forward to look at the picture, smiled up at Melissa, and said, "Patty's a beautiful partridge."

It didn't register in my brain at first. Then the words came tumbling out of my mouth. "She's a what? I thought she was a quail . . . or a bobwhite."

"A partridge," Cora Lee said.

"Yes, Patty's a partridge," Melissa said.

"Oh my gosh," I yelled, "that's it!"

Melissa looked up at me, puzzled but smiling. "What are you talking about, Jake?"

I tapped at my notebook, smiled back at Melissa, and said, "It's all in here, a count-down to where we can find Patty."

"Count down? What do you mean? Where's Patty?"

I tapped the first item on the page and said,

"*Twelve*, a drummer drumming.

"*Eleven*, the piper piping a water line.

'*Ten*, Lords a-leaping on their skateboards.

"*Nine*, ladies dancing.

"*Eight*, Cool Maids a-milking their customers.

"*Seven*, a swan a-swimming.

"*Six*, geese a-laying in the sun."

This is when Cora Lee chimed in with, "*Five* golden rings!"

"Yeah," I said, "*five* golden rings on the bar.

"*Four*, calling birds.

"*Three*, a French hen.

"*Two*, turtle doves.

Melissa threw her arms around my neck and said, "And my Patty *is in my pear tree!*" She stood up and raced to the door and the pear tree in her front yard.

And sure enough, there she was. Patty in the pear tree.

As Cora Lee says, sometimes silly can be really good.

CHAPTER 4
A SPIRITUAL CASE

There has always been something mesmerizing about watching my underwear fight each other in a laundromat dryer. My skivvies were winning because a heavy sock lost its energy through a hole in the toe. It was too much for my sensitive eyes, so I stood up to wander among the washers, dodging rug-rat toddlers and harried Mamas.

The bulletin board on the back wall is always entertaining for an active mind. Notices told me I could buy a term paper or hire a tutor. I could buy an old car or share driving on a trip to Chicago. Or, believe it or not, one blatant notice said I could date a girl named Suzanne, who loved lobster.

Jumping on the bandwagon, I pulled out my "Jake Whittaker, Private Investigations" card, found a free thumbtack, and pinned it at eye level. I moved back to the dryer and sat in a chair to see who was winning the underwear battle.

"Are you Jake Whittaker?" a voice behind me asked. I jerked around to see a latter-day Willie Nelson staring at me. He had long, scraggly hair and a craggy face covered by a gray beard. The way his shoulders slumped forward, I figured he had more problems than being middle aged.

I nodded.

He held out a hand and said, "I'm Dan Callahan. I saw you put your card on the wall." We were shaking hands as he added, "Do you work with frauds?"

I couldn't help but smile. "I really prefer my clients are honest," I said.

"No, I mean can you prove to my wife that our dead son isn't really talking to her though the medium she's been seeing?"

"Whoa," I said, "I'm good at locating people who skip out on their bills or their families, but I go to a cemetery to find dead people."

"Do you believe that we really can contact the dead?"

"Hell no, it's hard enough talking to the living. Besides, shouldn't the dead have better things to do than talk to us who are still struggling with life?"

"Can you show my wife Barbara that her medium is a fraud?"

"Why? If it makes her feel good, what's the harm?"

He plunked down in the chair next to me. "I don't want to sound crass," he said, "but maybe my wife will think again about things like laundry instead of moping around until the next time she can contact our son. I miss Harry as much as she does, but we just don't have the kind of money this is costing us. I need someone to put a stop to it. She won't listen to me."

The word "money" reminded me that my daily need for it usually exceeds my income, and here was a way to fatten my wallet a little. What the hell, why not give it a whirl.

He didn't wince at my per diem plus expenses, and we shook hands on it. However, he only gave me two twenties as a retainer, but I rationalized that away because a hungry stomach was telling me it was past lunchtime. Luckily my pocket notebook hadn't gone through the wash this time, so I got the info I needed before we arranged for me to meet his wife that evening. I was to pretend I am a possible convert to the séance she would be attending. She would be expecting me at a coffee shop. The whole idea was rather sappy, but what the hell. I certainly wasn't above lying.

My clean, folded underwear was back in the third file drawer of my office/home long before I headed out for a coffee shop on the near west side where I'd agreed to meet Dan's wife Barbara. I didn't have the slightest idea if my sport shirt made me look like a happy balance between a businessman and a guy seeking to talk to someone in the hereafter. Somehow the darkness of the evening seemed apropos.

★★★

I parked my jalopy down the street from the coffee shop. The only woman sitting alone was in a booth next to a large window. I walked up and said, "Are you Barbara?" She nodded and motioned for me to sit opposite her.

"I'm Jake," I said.

She was a typical matron, with heavy stockings, a skirt that covered her knees, cheeks bright red with rough, and hair that looks like curlers had just been removed.

"Thanks for giving me the opportunity to see Madame Corona," I said. "Does she live around here?"

She pointed out the window to a small building across the street. It looked like a commercial building that had gone residential. "Right there," she said. There was no sign on the building, just a street number.

"Will she accept someone new?" I asked.

"Oh sure. Everyone is welcome as long as they're a believer."

Oh sure, as long as they're a believer whose pockets are lined with green, I thought.

"How much does Madame cost?"

"Fifty dollars a session, but your first time is free." *Fifty bucks a head? I thought. Damn, I was in the wrong racket.*

We ordered coffee and compared notes about each other, each telling who we missed who had "passed on" to a supposedly better life. I mentioned my beloved Granny. Why not.

By the time our cups were empty, we were smiling with compassion at each other and ready to see Madame Corona. We walked silently across the street.

"You're gonna love Madame Corona," Barbara said. I figured someone named after a beer had to have something going for her.

Barbara lifted a huge brass knocker on the building's door. The door had the good humor to actually creak when it opened, conjuring up visions of gothic castles. A silent boy in a St. Catherine's uniform waved us inside, and our heels clumped over Mexican tiles as we followed him to a room covered—walls, ceiling, and floor—with square-foot pieces of carpeting in a multitude of colors. I made a mental note of how contrasting colors and seams could hide thin wires and paraphernalia.

In the middle of the room wooden, high-back chairs surrounded a round pedestal table with a wide horizontal edge. *That edge,* I thought, *will keep anyone from seeing under the table.* One upholstered chair was larger than the others and had deep folds in the fabric. Everything about the room screamed "fraud!"

I hoped skepticism didn't show on my face as I was introduced to Madame Corona. She was the perfect stereotype of a medium, complete with a long skirt, large hoop earrings, Birkenstock sandals, and rings on most of her fingers. She was obviously a graduate of gypsy school, but it was her eyes that sucked away disbelief. A mother doe couldn't have managed a softer, more sincere look. Her friendly smile said welcome, and her callused hands said she worked at something besides entertaining spirits from the netherworld. I was intrigued and anxious at the same time. Anxious for what, I didn't know.

"I sense the spirits will be with you tonight," she said to me. "You sit here next to me. I'll guide you through." *Through what?* "Is there a loved one you want to get in touch with this evening?"

Just as I was about to answer, the door opened and three other people came in, guided by St. Catherine's Uniform. Madame Corona made the introductions. One was a schoolteacher type named Victoria who wore a no-nonsense pants suit and the hairdo my mother gave up when I was in seventh grade. Dotty was a female who had just reached the age when "woman" sounds more descriptive than "girl." Mr. Whipple, the only other man, had coke-bottle glasses and a button-down shirt. They all looked anxious and interested, so I kept a close rein on showing my disbelief.

Everyone found a seat. I lowered myself into the chair between Barbara and the large, padded chair, which was obviously meant for Madame Corona. After twirling the knob on a switch to dim the overhead light, Madame slid into her chair without even moving it. When she put both hands palms up on the table, the others immediately complied, grasping the hands next to them. I followed suit, completing the circle. At least Madame wasn't about to perform any sleight of hand.

"Do not break the circle of love," she said. When she spoke again, her voice sounded like a preacher at a funeral service. "We have come here tonight in love and faith," she said, "and we come in sorrow and grief for those who have moved on ahead of us. We need to know that life beyond this world is happy and safe. Those who have made the journey know what we so desperately want to know, so again we call upon our beloved Carlos to speak to us from the spirit world, to guide us to those we once cherished in this temporal life."

Who the hell was Carlos? The kid in uniform?

She closed her eyes and tilted her head back. "Beloved Carlos, we call you to leave your spirit world and join us at our table. Let us know that you are with us."

I couldn't help but smile, but it was wiped away by a knocking sound on the underside of the table, and Barbara's hand gripped mine tighter in anticipation. As I glanced around the table, all hands were in sight, and I began to feel a little edgy.

Madame's head was still tilted toward the ceiling. "Speak to us, I beg you," she chanted. When nothing happened, she called out again in a slightly angry voice, "Carlos, where are you?"

The disembodied voice that came back sounded out of breath, or maybe it was just very spiritual. "I'm here. I'm here," the deep voice said, but I couldn't see Madame's lips move. My guess was that she had an accomplice who was a little slow on the draw or else she was a damn good ventriloquist. Whatever, I was beginning to be impressed.

"Carlos, do you think Miss Ventura could speak to her mother again?" The schoolteacher type across the table sucked in her breath.

"She's pruning her roses and doesn't want to be bothered," the voice of Carlos said.

"Mama loves her flowers!" This was from Miss Ventura.

"Please, Carlos, just ask her," Madame begged.

It was quiet around the table with no words from either world, real or spiritual. Madame twisted her head from side to side, as though relieving a crick in her neck, until there was another quick tap on the underside of the table. It was an older, female voice this time. "The Crimson Glories aren't as thick this year. Victoria, have you been messing with my roses again?" Obviously, it was Mama from the great beyond.

Victoria Ventura slumped down in her chair, gripping the hands beside her even tighter. "Of course not," she said. "How could I?"

"Sit up straight!" Mama commanded. Victoria's spine became a ramrod, and Mama almost shouted, "Are you still seeing that silly math teacher?" Even in the dim light I could see Victoria's face blush.

Victoria changed the subject. "Mama," she said, "I need your recipe for pot roast. Yours was always the best."

"Humph! Try Betty Crocker, but if you're cooking for you-know-who, he only wants the inheritance I left you. Didn't I tell you men are no good?"

Victoria slumped down in her chair again and said, "Oh Mama!"

"All right, Victoria, go make your love offering. I have to get back to my roses." I almost imagined Mama walking, back to some nether land. I mentally shook my head and waited.

After a moment's silence there was another rap under the table. I wanted to duck my head to see what was going on under there but couldn't with my hands held by those beside me.

Then Carlos was back. "There's someone here who wants to talk to Jake," he said.

Damn! I found myself holding my breath right in the middle of my disbelief.

"Jakie?" a soft voice said. Only my grandmother had called me that!

"That you, Grandma?" I think I was just playing along, but I also felt like I was following Alice down the rabbit hole.

"Yes, son." It was an easy guess. "Have you been a good boy? Are you saving your money and watching it grow?" I had to swallow. Do all grandmas say that, or was it just mine?

Even in my confusion, I decided to help Madame out. I wanted to see what she'd do with the mention of money. "That's the problem, Grandma," I said. "I need help on what investments to buy."

Madame's head jerked forward faster than a jolted electrician. She stared at me, and this time I could easily see her mouth as the voice started in again just before she flipped her face back to the ceiling. The words came from her spot at the table, but her lips weren't moving.

"I can help you, Jakie. Come back next week and I'll tell you what to buy," Grandma's voice said.

Then Carlos suddenly rapped again to let us know he was back, and we all listened to Mrs. Whipple talk to his dead wife who thought he was still Mr. Wonderful.

Finally Madame Corona let her head flop forward and said, "I'm sorry, that's all for tonight. The spirits take all my strength." Barbara dropped my hand and reached across me to pat Madame's hand. "It's all right," she said. "Maybe Harry will come talk to me next time." Madame's smile gave Barbara all the assurance she wanted. *Sure, you old fake,* I thought, *string 'em out at fifty bucks a crack* – or maybe it was more than that.

Before we left, everyone pressed money at Madame, but Mr. Whipple's was in a thick envelope. He surrounded both Madame's hands around the envelope, kissed her check, and thanked her like she was a saint.

I was impressed and disgusted at the same time. Maybe grandmas are special to everyone, but I didn't like mine exploited, even if it felt good to hear things my grandma said to me when I was little.

I left Barbara and drove to Frank's bar, back in my own element where the owner/bartender usually spoke with the raise of an eyebrow rather than words, and the pretzel bowls were quickly refilled. I nursed a beer through grandma-thoughts of bib aprons, chocolate brownies and nursery rhymes, bittersweet memories that remained with me until I later fell asleep on my office couch and dreamed youthful visions.

★★★

"Can I get a book on horses?" Cora Lee said. "Mama got me her library card."

We were on our way to the library so I could get a handle on spiritualists, mediums and séances. "Yeah, sure," I said, "but this is work for me, remember. You have to keep quiet and let me do my research."

"What are you looking for?"

"A way to tell someone that she can't talk to her son after he's dead."

"Why not? I sometimes talk to my Aunt Jenny who died last year."

Kids are full of way too many questions. I didn't have time to explain fraud to any eight-year-old and started to regret I'd agreed to take Cora Lee so Loretta and Donna could go to an action movie. This was getting to be too often. I swore to myself this was my last time with the kid.

"Look, kid," I said, "we can't expect the dead to talk back to us. It just ain't gonna happen."

Her mouth broke into a pout. "Mama says anything is possible."

"Did Mama also say you're way too smart for your own good? Did she, huh?" I turned to look at her briefly. We just smiled at each other.

Once we were in the library, I spent a lot of time in one of their easy chairs, even falling asleep at one point. But I also got a quick lesson on the book catalog and only went to ask for further assistance three times, partly because the reference librarian had a quirky smile and the legs of a gazelle. She was also patient to a newcomer who didn't even know Dewey had developed his own library system long before he lost the election to Truman. By the time I'd found my pile of books, I had warm feelings for librarians and soft, upholstered chairs. All in all, it was a good rewarding afternoon.

★★★

I was well informed when I met Barbara again outside Madame's place a few days later, ready to confront Madame and Carlos. St. Catherine's Uniform was looking surly, and Madame Corona seemed angry at the same time she sweetly bid us welcome. It looked like Madame's family hadn't contacted the spirit of domestic tranquility on this particular day.

We had some different people this time. Victoria probably hadn't been up to facing her mother again, and Mr. Whipple must have been satisfied after his last session with his dear departed wife.

Rainy was new. She reminded me of a pumpkin with her green spiky hair and a short orange crop top, except that she was so thin she would probably disappear if viewed from the side.

Jonathan had nerd written all over him. He wore those narrow end-of-the-nose drugstore glasses. He tried to keep his distance from Rainy like he was afraid she had a social disease.

Me? I was armed with my library knowledge and ready to do battle. However, I kept my disbelief to myself and hoped it didn't show.

Madame seemed in a hurry. This time she collected the fees up front, and I reluctantly forked over fifty bucks, glad I could put it on my expense account. Madame waved us somewhat impatiently toward the chairs and drastically dimmed the lights before taking her place at the table. I sat opposite her, between Jonathan and Rainy, with my chair not too close to the table. Barbara scooted up closer to Madame like she was anxious to be noticed by the voice of Carlos when he left his busy schedule long enough to play intermediary. Oh yeah, I was full of new knowledge about spiritualism. I knew all the buzzwords.

With our hands joined around the table, Madame began by admonishing us that any disbelief could "fragment" the spirits, whatever that means. Then she chanted, "Caaarlos, Caaarlos," evidentially calling to both of his fragments.

It took a moment for the knocking to sound under the table, Carlos letting us know he'd arrived. Madame's head was thrown back again, and it gave me a chance to lean back as far as I could to see that her feet were out of the Birkenstocks and several toes had rings on them. If microphone and speaker wires were involved, I couldn't see them in that light.

The hands on either side of me tightened when Carlos groaned his presence. He seemed as impatient as Madame. "Okay, who do you want?" he blurted out.

I saw Madame's hand squeeze Barbara's. "Can you bring Harry to us, please, Carlos? His mother is right here by my side."

"Harry, huh? Let me see if he's available." There was a pause for a moment before he added, "We have other things to do, you know. Heaven isn't all fun and games."

"Heaven!" Barbara said. "My Harry is in heaven? He never told me that before."

I could have sworn I heard Carlos groan in disgust before silence fell on the room.

"Hi, Mom," a husky voice said. I wondered if Madame Corona had this low a range in her voice. It didn't sound like St. Catherine's Uniform speaking this time. His adolescent voice would work for Carlos but maybe not for an adult Larry. Maybe there was a Mr. Corona working in the background.

Barbara sucked in her breath before saying, "Hi, Baby."

"Mom, I'm not a baby."

"I know, sweetie, but your Dad and I sure miss you." When Harry didn't answer, she went on. "Carlos says you're in heaven. Tell me what it's like."

Well, all right. There wasn't going to be a closed ear at the table. I wanted to hear Harry's story, too, even if I knew it came from the vivid mind of a live person.

"I no longer have cancer up here, Mom. And there won't be any down there either when Dr. Duncan finishes his research."

"Who's Dr. Duncan?"

"A scientist Madame Corona knows about. His research is almost there, Mom. A cure, a real cure for cancer. He just needs a little more money."

Jonathan looked uncertain, and Rainy shook her head in disbelief. Okay, Madame, I thought, just how do you explain Harry knowing about what some guy named Duncan is doing down here?

Barbara just said, "But how . . .?"

Madame had to notice the shift in confidence that had crept into the room.

"Are you sure about that?" Barbara said. "A real cure?" The question seemed to defuse the impossibility of Harry's knowledge. Even I wondered what Harry would say next.

"I really wasn't supposed to tell you," Harry's voice said, "but talk to Madame Corona. She'll tell you." Before anyone could react to that, he said, "Carlos says I have to go now," and I could almost imagine him floating away as surely as if he'd turned his spiritual back and disappeared into the cosmos.

All through the rest of the séance I tried to get a handle on Madame's con and had to admire a fraud who would bring an uncertain group back into the fold so easily. I barely listened as Rainy talked to a boyfriend who'd OD'd on heroin, but I wasn't too surprised Madame knew the drug jargon. Jonathan asked to talk to his ex-partner, but as soon as the appropriate voice showed up, Jonathan abruptly got up from the table and slammed out of the room. It obviously hadn't been a congenial partnership.

It also broke the circle. The séance was ended, and Madame was obviously peeved. She's been out of sorts when we arrived, but now she was quietly seething. She waved the rest of us out into the hallway to leave. At the same time she pulled Barbara aside. I waited in my car outside, staring at the door until Barbara came out fifteen minutes later.

I quickly got out of my car and followed her to hers. "Okay, let's have it," I said, as I caught up to her as she was opening her car.

"It's not your business," she said. "It's between my son and me."

"No, it's not. It's between you, the greedy Madame Corona, and the non-existent Dr. Duncan."

Her look was hard as she slid into the driver's seat, closed the car door, and opened the window. "There is too a Dr. Duncan. Madame's going to introduce me to him at his lab as soon as he has the time. He's working on a cure that will save other young people like my Harry." She started the engine. "So leave us alone, Mr. Whittaker. I don't care if you are one of Dan's clients."

I was bungling badly. I was angry with myself for treating her like a nitwit who believed in the tooth fairy, and I was angry with her for not seeing Madame as the Wizard of Con. It was time to hedge a little. I said, "Barbara, I'm sorry. I know it isn't any of my business, but I have a feeling you're about to do something even your son would feel bad about."

She turned on the motor and looked up at me. It was time to come clean. "Look," I said, "Dan sent me to go with you to Madame's, because he's worried about you. He loved your son, and he loves you." Tears began to form in her eyes. "Go with Madame to see this Dr. Duncan if you must, but for everyone's sake, don't make any decisions about money until we can talk again." Her lips pursed. "Please," I added.

She reached down, ready to close the window. "Okay," she said, "you can come with me to the special séance Madame is having tomorrow night, but I don't make any promises about anything." Then she rolled up the window and drove off.

I breathed a sigh, walked back to my car, and headed for Frank's place to do my own spiritual communication. As usual, Frank didn't say one word as he served me my beer and I listened to the echo of thoughts rattling around in my brain until it was time to go home.

★★★

I popped a warm can of Coke Classic and leaned back in my desk chair to think. First I addressed the tapping noise under the séance table that signaled Carlos' arrival. I tried bringing my shoe up to tap against the underside of my desk. It sounded like a shoe hitting a desk, not like a spirit rapping for attention. Besides, Madame had taken her shoes off during the last séance. I took one shoe off and tried knocking my toes under the desk. My stomach muscles strained to raise my leg that high, and I only managed one swing and one bang. No rap, rap, rap.

I tried rapping the tops of my toes against the file drawer side of the desk. Rap, rap. Weak, but definitely a rap. Madame Corona had youth and practice on her side, and she also had those rings on her toes. I was satisfied with that.

One trick was solved, but I still wasn't sure about both male and female voices coming from Madame's place at the table. For the next few minutes I tried out different voices at the same time I tried to keep my lips from moving. It was an embarrassing failure.

But then I remembered St. Catherine's Uniform being out of sorts at our last session. I remembered Madame trying to hide her own anger and Carlos being impatient when called out from his spiritual tranquility. I was forced to believe Madame had a family connected to the séance room by microphone and speaker wires.

Ideas began to form in my mind. I pictured the electronic display in the window of Over-&-Easy Pawn Shop. I smiled. Two could play at this game.

I managed to find enough money in pants pockets to back my plan. Grandma would have liked the swagger in my walk as I locked up the office and headed for Over-&-Easy on the street below.

★★★

Barbara was barely cordial when we met in the hallway outside Madame Corona's the next night. She might listen to son Harry but she didn't want to listen to anything more I had to say. At least she didn't blow my cover.

We went inside and joined the others.

Rainy was back and Victoria was ready to give her mother another try, but I was too antsy to listen to any of the talk around me. I was about to pay my dues in the Actors' Guild with a script I'd only practiced once.

Show time, I said to myself as Madame dimmed the lights to a new low and slid into her special chair without moving it an inch. I knew there were a microphone and a speaker somewhere in the dark folds of fabric surrounding the back of her chair. I knew we were both glad that visibility was poor. But I also knew my shoes were equipped with taps Fred Estaire would envy, my body was wired with the best electronics my money could borrow, and my elbow was waiting patiently for its cue.

We all grabbed the hand of those sitting next to us. Madame Corona leaned her head into the back of her chair and stared at the ceiling, the smile on her face telling me this was a better day in her household than last time. I was about to wipe the smile away, and hopefully get Barbara to understand that her son Harry should live on in her heart, not through the greedy manipulations of a fake.

It was only seconds before the Carlos tapping sounded beneath the table. "Caaarlos," Madame chanted, and then she added, "Mr. Whittaker is back with us again. Is there anyone out there who wishes to speak to him?"

"Oh yes!" a female voice said. My heart almost stopped. The voice wasn't familiar, but the way she spoke sounded familiar. "Oh yes," said in just that way I remembered Joleen had always said. Bittersweet memories of years ago flooded over me. I saw Joleen with me on a porch swing and remembered my amazement at having won the heart of the most wonderful girl I've ever known. My mind saw our wedding plans dissolve into her funeral. I shivered. Even knowing I wasn't actually hearing from Joleen, I was thankful the dim lighting hid my face from the others.

"*Joleen?*" my voice said, without my permission.

"Yes, it's me."

"That isn't your voice."

"Our voices change when our bodies change," the voice said. "I have a whole healthy body now." Yeah, it was something I wanted to believe, but I didn't.

"Why didn't you ever marry, Jake?"

Not even I knew all the reasons why. At the moment I knew nothing except the fast beating of my heart as I shook my head.

Then in the space of several seconds my mind fished for Madame Corona's source of knowledge. I'd stupidly given her my real name. If she started with that, she could have searched newspaper archives for engagement announcements, obituaries, and any number of documents that showed I'd never been married. She knew how to do her homework. She probably also knew I was a P.I., but evidentially she didn't care.

"I never found another Joleen," I said.

Before the supposed Joleen could speak again, I got my act together. The tap on my left shoe clicked loudly against the underside of the table. Madame Corona's head jerked down to see that all our hands were still joined on top of the table. Good, I'd caught her off guard.

My elbow pushed and held a switch on my right side. "Hold it!" a voice strangely like mine said, but my mouth was tightly closed. Every head at the table snapped to look in my direction. Perfect! "This women is a fake!" the voice continued before I let up on the switch.

"What's going on?" Madame called out. "Carlos?"

"Beats the hell out of me," the voice of Carlos said, and it definitely wasn't Madame talking.

"Ah shit!" Rainy said. "I might have known!"

Victoria groaned and dropped the hands of those beside her.

Barbara had the beginnings of disbelief on her face as she said, "What's happening here, Madame?"

"This séance is over," Madame said. "Evil spirits are trying to take over. They are saying wicked things. God will not stand for this sacrilege."

That did it! Bringing Joleen into this mess was one thing; claiming sacrilege was going a little too far.

I pushed in again with my elbow. This time it was a female voice that came out of the folds of my shirt. "Whatever you want is what you'll get," it said.

"What the hell?" Madame said. She was definitely out of character. She didn't recognize the slogan of the sandwich shop two blocks from my office where a clerk had repeated it for me as she made my sandwich last night. The words weren't quite in context, but it did show a female as well as a male voice.

By this time no one was holding anyone else's hand. Everyone slumped down in the chairs, and heads were shaking.

My elbow again hit its mark. The male voice in my shirt said, "Voices can easily come through wires from another room."

"No!" Madame said. "We are alone except for my son in the kitchen. Go see for yourself!" It sounded more like a command for confederates to flee than an explanation to us. When no one moved, she looked around the table. "Who's talking?" she said. It was too late. The disbelief in the room was thick.

I couldn't remember what I'd programmed next on the recording, but I elbowed the next words anyway. The voice on the recording said, "She only wants your money." Things were apt to get out of context if I kept the recorder rolling, so I counted my blessings and called it a day.

Madame stood up, still careful to not move her chair. "I said this séance is over," she demanded. "You must all leave now. Evil has taken over, and the good spirits will no longer enter this room." She was angry, knowing that she would have to find all new people to bamboozle. Then revenge put an angry look on her face. "You shall never again, any of you, speak with your dear departed ones."

The faces of the others getting up from the table didn't look disappointed; they just looked sad. We all left the house in silence, each with our own thoughts—except Rainy who kept saying, "Shit, shit, shit." It was apropos.

Barbara didn't pull away when I took her arm and led her to a small café on the corner. I figured my expense account could cover an after-theater meal. It wasn't until the waitress had taken our order that Barbara began with her questions. I showed her the recorder on my belt. I told her Madame had her own electronic equipment in that padded chair. It seems no one had ever seen a husband or any other children but St. Catherine's Uniform, but assumptions could be made.

I knew I had earned my fee when Barbara said, "But I liked talking to Harry, even if it was only a voice from the kitchen."

"I know," I said. I didn't tell her I'd liked talking to Joleen, too.

CHAPTER 5
A SHAGGY DOG CASE

He pushed open the door marked "Jake Whittaker, Private Investigations," and his ego swaggered across my office with a hand held out. "I'm Freddy Contrees," he said. I knew I was shaking hands with a hyper-attitude problem.

He swept dust off my client chair before lowering himself into it and rested his arms on his stomach shelf. He stared at me and raked his tongue across his lower lip, giving me time to take in the gold jewelry and alligator boots. It also gave me time to wonder why such a well-heeled jerk came to a P.I. whose office doubled as his home.

"What can I do for you, Mr. Contrees?"

He tried to smile, but it came out as just over-confident. "I own Plebeian Publishing," he said, "a laid-back shop that dabbles in a little of everything."

I leaned forward in my chair. "You mean you're not above selling porn."

"Hey, don't snub your righteous nose, Whittaker. We print whatever John Q. Public will buy, and that includes biographies, cookbooks, and even poetry."

He tried to stare me down. I let him, because I remembered my overdue rent. I turned on my nice talk, even if I don't touch porn with asbestos gloves. "And how do I fit into the picture?" I said. "I don't cook, and reading my life story would work faster than a sleeping pill."

He flashed a gaudy ring as his hand waved away my words. "Someone in my organization is making off with part of my profits. After a bumper quarter in sales, our profits dipped eight points. And I don't share my bottom line with anyone but my wife's credit card companies."

"What do you need from me?"

"I need you to find out who's got off-shore accounts that should be in my name."

My eyes rolled up into my head. "Oh sure, I come around asking questions, and the thief is going to open right up and confess."

"I'll bring you into the shop as an editor. You get acquainted with who has the sticky fingers, and I'll take it from there."

"What kind of editor?"

Contrees picked at a fingernail for a moment. "How about true crime? There's always a market for the truth."

I coughed to cover a belly laugh, but then I warmed up to the idea. At least my landlord would be happy I finally had some money coming in. I stated my terms, and he shrugged in agreement. With this client, though, a handshake wasn't going to cut it, so I pulled out a form, filled in the blanks, and pushed it across the desk for him to sign. After nailing down some details, we agreed I'd begin the following morning. I just hoped Plebeian Publishing didn't get raided while I was a pseudo-employee.

★★★

"This is Kevin Beals," Contrees sad, "jack-of-all-trades and my right-hand problem solver."

I couldn't help but compare myself to Beals. His khaki pants had creases that could have shaved his legs. My pants just bag. His turtleneck was black and tight fitting, but it didn't have my pullover's little alligator. He was cabana handsome; I like to think of myself as cottage cute. When his handshake showed he worked out, I quit wanting to make comparisons.

Before he left us, Contrees said, "Get him started, Kevin. I want Whittaker to get acquainted before I turn him loose."

"You one of the editors?" I asked Beals.

"I oversee the books no one wants to talk about."

"Porn, huh?"

"The soft stuff. But I do a lot of trade books about which bars in town cater to special needs and what restaurants titillate the psyche." When he got no reaction from me, he added, "Tell you what. I'll get you started meeting our people, and later I'll take you to one of my favorite places for lunch." His smile showed satisfaction as he said, "You're gonna love The Cowgirl."

He introduced me to the cookbook editor's secretary, Margarette, but I doubt she caught my name. All her attention was on Beals. He smiled at her with perfect teeth, making me wonder how much he spent just on his mouth. He left the two of us alone with a promise to catch up with me for lunch—and a promise in his eyes to Margarette that dripped testosterone.

Margarette looked at her watch before pointing toward a door. "Go on in," she said. "Dorothy . . . hmmm, Ms. Brooks . . . has twenty-two minutes to talk. She has a flan in the oven."

A flan in the oven? What the hell is a flan? Was that another way of saying she was pregnant? I nodded my head like I knew what a flan was, gave a brief knock on the door, and went on in.

Dorothy Brooks' domain was half office and half kitchen. Figuring only the older generation still knew how many cups are in a quart, I expected to see a knock-off of my granny in a bib apron. Not so. Brooks had a little of my granny's girth and a fair portion of her final age, but she was surprisingly sophisticated in an expensive suit and a casual hair style that only a large pocketbook could afford. I introduced myself as a new editor and asked, "You cook? I thought you were an editor."

She smiled as her hand waved at the small kitchen. "A perk and a responsibility. I have to check out my authors."

"How are the *money* perks around here? I doubt if I can afford whiskey on the beer salary I'll be getting."

She leaned in and whispered to me. "You look smart, Jake. It won't take you long to figure out about taking a non-existent author to lunch. You play it right, your pockets get a little fatter." Her raised eyebrows weren't exactly editorial.

She checked her watch and said, "Listen, Honey, I've got work to do, but drop in any time you want." The words might have been my grandmother's, but the underlying message definitely wasn't. I was being dismissed.

I'm not sure what I mumbled on my way out. I was too busy grieving over latter-day grandmotherly types.

Margarette was on the phone, so I pulled out my pocket notebook and noted Dorothy Brooks as a suspect. For someone who spent time reading cookbooks, she just may have been cooking up a scheme of her own. Non-existent authors could be a lucrative scam—and another reason to pad her wallet..

As I wandered down the hall past other secretaries outside other office doors, I wondered what really went on around here and found myself humming *"Behind Closed Doors."* When I hit the end of the hall, I backtracked to an office marked Arthur B. Dresser. Instead of a secretary there was a table full of paperwork, piles and piles. The first group I looked at had a heading that said Balance Sheet. Well, it seemed to be very still and balancing.

Just then I heard the sound of breaking glass and jerked my eyes toward the office door. I knocked, but all I heard was someone yelling, "Damn! My lucky cup!"

I took that for a "come in" and eased into a room that looked like a paper depository, filled to the brim with banks of file cabinets and a desk piled high with more stacks of paper. I suddenly realized a lot of trees had died. I didn't see anyone until a head poked up from behind the desk with a hand holding a cup handle without a cup. "This is worse than five years for breaking a mirror," the head said. "Now nothing will go right. I just know it." The long face sagged even more as he got up and slumped into a chair.

My explanation about being a new editor seemed to sink into his mind, but he was still holding the cup handle as we shook hands. "Don't tell me," I said, my eyes sweeping around the room. "You're the money tracker of this operation."

"I'm the treasurer. More like the only perfectionist in this shitty rat hole."

"Strong words."

He threw the cup handle down with the rest of the broken cup. "Ah hell, the pay's good—if you know how to play the odds—but getting these dudes to give me *all* the paperwork I need, *when* I need it, is harder than hitting the exacta at the track last Saturday.

"You must have bet on Baker's Dozen in the third, right?" That nag hadn't been good to me, either.

He nodded and looked down, as unhappy as a second cousin who wasn't mentioned in the will. Then he shrugged and looked back down at his feet. "It was my lucky cup!" He was quiet and I realized I was no longer a part of his present time.

I left him staring down at the pieces of broken cup he was sure meant his life had come to an end.

I thought how silly it was for anyone to be that superstitious, even as I softly knocked for good luck on the wood trim of the next door I passed..

In the hallway I added Arthur B. Dresser to my notebook. A money man who bets on the nags is as suspect as a food editor who might just cooks up bogus costs on an expense account.

The sign on the next office door had so many names, I thought it might be a boy's dormitory, except one of the names was definitely female. I pictured the room I'd shared as a kid with my brothers, so I barged into this room without knocking and stood in the open doorway. The room had one desk and four long banquet tables against the far walls, each one a different color. A guy in horn-rimmed glasses looked at me in surprise and said, "The men's room is two doors down."

"Sorry," I muttered. "I'm Jake Whittaker, the new true crime editor." I pointed to the names on the door. "Which one are you? I moved forward to shake his hand.

"All of them." There was a smirk on his face.

"Split personality—or unable to live on only one paycheck?" This time it was my turn to smirk.

He held out a hand. "I'm Josh Phelps when I've visiting my mother and when I'm the editor of Plebeian's how-to books. I'm Janet Cleaver when I'm the writer of household hints. As the editor of craft books, I'm Jeremy Handy. And I use the name Justin Dooit for the self-help books I either edit or write.

"How do you balance all those things?"

"You obviously haven't read Janet Cleaver's *Clever Control Conceptions.*"

Hell, I hadn't even read John Grisham. I shook my head.

He waved me over toward the colored tables. The red one had piles of typewritten pages and long sheets of printed pages that looked like books in progress. "Color coded," he said proudly. He grinned and said, "This table is red because all these have to be read!" I groaned as his hand waved at the piles of pages. "They're manuscripts and galley sheets," he added.

He grabbed my arm and pulled me to the next table. "This white table is where I work on household hints books. White for clean!"

He moved on to a brown table as I got into the color thing and said, "And brown is because . . . ?"

"Because I have to edit all the *shitty* crafts books. They may be my bread and butter, but who the hell cares except the leisure-time ladies who don't have anything better to do?"

I was no longer willing to second-guess the blue table, so I just pointed to it with a question in my eyes.

"Self-help," he said.

I allowed the question to remain on my face.

"Some are exercise books that make you black and blue, so I settled for blue. Some are books to perk up blue spirits. And then there're the books to teach any skills I might pull 'out of the blue.' " I pretended like it made sense.

"Such as?" I asked.

"Such as my newest, *Wealth Without Work*."

I smiled. "Sounds like good work if you can find it."

He allowed a small grin to show up on his face. "I'm very resourceful," he said. "It's a crime how easy wealth can come when you know how to work it—or *not* work it if you read the book." With little more than a hesitation, he added, "And now I better get back to my work and let you get to yours."

I was again dismissed as surely as a school bell signaling the end of class. As his office door closed behind me, I stood in the hallway and wrote Josh Phelp's name in my notebook, along with a notation to get a copy of *Wealth Without Work*. It probably wouldn't give a clue to how stealing might be done at Plebeian Publishing, but maybe it could show me a way to pay my outstanding bill at Frank's bar.

★★★

Noon rolled around, and I followed Kevin Beals into The Cowgirl restaurant. Beals was right; I liked the place right from the start. Young, sexy girls in short cowgirl outfits were slinging beer mugs and lunch plates at customers. Cool beer and warm bodies. This was the first thing all day I really appreciated. It was obviously a place only a guy with a libido and an expense account could afford.

Beals was obviously well known here. Three cowgirls broke into smiles and motioned for us to sit at one of the tables they served. He chose one, and a fringed cowgirl outfit bounced over, stood inches from Beals, and crooned, "Two beers?" She didn't acknowledge me, even with my good manners tuned up and ready to play her song. Neither did he. I doubt if anyone would have noticed me even if I'd been nude. I slumped down and read the menu printed on the paper placemat. I could have my choice of steak any way I wanted it, as long as I wanted it costly.

While devouring a surprisingly good steak sandwich a few minutes later, I watched Beals smile and call everyone by name. But I was content when a second fresh frosty beer mug appeared in front of me before I'd even asked.

Before we headed back to Plebeian, Beals pulled out a fat wallet and overpaid the check as our cowgirl leaned her bosom far out over the table and giggled. Goose bumps raised on my arms, and I had to sit on my hands to keep them from reacting.

When I was left alone again in the publishing office, I took out my pocket notebook and entered Beals' name. No one struggling and honest has a wallet full of greenbacks in these days. No one on salary, albeit the number two man, has female anatomy leaning over him without having more than a pretty face.

With that thought, I steeled myself for boredom and knocked at a door with a sign saying "The Poet's Corner."

A neutral voice said, "All right."

What the hell did that mean? I stood there silently until the door was opened by a good-looking person who reminded me of a schoolteacher I'd once had a crush on. The person standing in the doorway had loose pants and a tailored jacket, short but wavy hair and thick glasses. The problem was, it could have been a man; it could have been a woman. It was eerie not being sure.

I played it safe. "I'm Jake Whittaker," I said. "I'm the new true crime editor. You're . . .?"

"Pat Gnomes . . . poetry." The first name was no help. Neither was the voice. I shrugged inwardly and pretended it made no difference. Nor did it make a difference to Pat that the first question I blurted out was, "Do people still read poetry?"

"Of course. From limericks to sonnets to country songs. Free verse or rhymes, metered or rambling."

"I never got past 'Now I lay me down to sleep.'"

Pat smiled. "Little Jack Horner was my favorite."

I looked around the office, the first one without clutter and confusion. No colorful tables, no piles of manuscripts, no financial papers. "Is there money in poetry?" I asked. "Can an editor make a living out of it?"

"Sadly, no. Even Will Shakespeare had to double as an actor. Poets don't fare much better today. But Mr. Contrees lets me plug on."

"Why? I don't see Contrees doing anything that doesn't add to his bank account."

After a moment's hesitation, Pat said, "Because, if you must know, I can also write really dirty limericks. Mr. Contrees knows the markets."

I broke into a smile. ". . . There was an old man from Nantucket . . . "

"Exactly!"

We both laughed.

"Maybe poetry does have its place," I said. "Maybe there is 'rhyme or reason' to it." The remark made me feel rather smug. Pat raised an eyebrow, to tell me the remark was appreciated. Was she/he coming on to me? Damn, I wanted to know if I was looking at a man or a woman.

Gnomes said, "Our food editor, Dorothy Brooks, tells me, 'We are what we eat.' I like to think we are what we read. And I think we tend to be called who we are."

I was fishing around for a retort when the door opened and Mr. Contrees stuck his head in. "Whittaker, got a minute? I'm sure Pat will excuse you." Pat Gnomes and I shook hands before I left, but the hand's skin and grip told me nothing. Some P.I. I turned out to be. I couldn't even figure out if the poetry editor was a he or a she.

But I did feel the nibble of a clue about this case trying to surface in my mind, but Contrees leading me down the hall chased it away.

"What's up?" I asked Contrees, once we got to his office.

"You're costing me by the hour," he said. "I want to know what kind of progress you're making." He pointed for me to sit as he sank into a leather chair behind a desk full of gold-plated accessories. Even his Rolodex had gold trim. "Who's the culprit?" he said. "How is my bottom line disappearing?"

I couldn't resist first giving him the truth as I saw it. I swept a hand in his direction. "In the first place," I said, "your bottom line appears to be disappearing into furnishings and indulgences." My hand waved toward things outside his office. "It's disappearing into perfect smiles and lady friends, into non-existent client expenses, and into wealth obtained without working."

He didn't take it well. "Well, in the first place, Whittaker, how I spend my money in my own company is damn well none of your business. And in the second place, do you have facts to back up any accusations you have, or are you guessing? I hired you to find a thief, not to give me a stupid, silly business prognosis."

Silly? The word brought two things to my mind. I remembered Cora Lee telling me it was okay to be silly sometimes. I remembered Pat Gnomes saying, "We tend to be called who we are." *Okay, I told myself, so you're silly — but you still get things done, Whittaker.*

My notebook was still in one hand, and I tapped it against my other hand. I knew the clues were right there in my notebook and in my head. I continued to look at Contrees, but my mind was whirling. Tap, tap tap . . .

Suddenly I did know who the Plebeian culprit was.

"That's quite a . . . person . . . you have in Pat Gromes," I told Contrees. "Pat let me know there can be 'rhyme and reason' in how to think."

"Yeah, yeah, great limericks. But who's draining me dry?"

Ignoring his question, I tapped my notebook again. "Well," I said, "Pat tells me we tend to be called who we are. Around here there is rhyme and reason to Plebeian's true crime." It was going a little overboard, but I couldn't resist.

"What the hell are you talking about, Whittaker?"

"The *reason* is in the *rhyme.* Let me see if I can lay this out for you so you'll understand." I started a run down:

"For instance," I said, "Dorothy Brooks is the one who cooks."

His expression showed he wasn't with me, but I went on anyway.

"*Arthur B. Dresser is the data processor.*"

Realization began to cross his face.

"*Josh Phelps does the self-helps.*"

As his head cocked to one side, I refrained from calling him *Contrees The Slease* and instead said, "*Pat Gnomes writes poems.*"

By this time he was fully with me. I said, "Beals spends more money than I assume lines up with his salary, so . . ."

He finished it by yelling, "So Beals is the one who steals!" Case closed.

CHAPTER 6
SADIE

She wasn't your usual grandma. The trim, gray-haired woman running down the sidewalk was wearing Reeboks and stretchy pants. The racing stripe down the side of the pants matched the bright pink flowers in her shirt, and even her socks were a gaudy pink. If I weren't a gentleman, I might have wondered about the color of her underwear.

She was only slightly out of breath when she stopped running and stepped in front of me as I started up the steps leading to my office/home. "You're Whittaker, aren't you?" she said.

"Yes, Ma'am. Jake Whittaker. Do I know you?"

She held out a hand. "Sadie Harrison. Call me Sadie. I live in Flat A over the flower shop.

I smiled and said something inane, wondering what she had in mind. She began jogging in place. "Be at my place in 40 minutes," she said.

"Ma'am . . . ?"

"I just finished frosting cinnamon rolls, and the coffee's hot. So is the story I need your help with." I must have looked confused. "Please," she added. Then she gave me a look that melted my resolve. She bounced for two more beats, looked pleadingly at me, and took off down the street, stretchy pants and all.

Guess where I was thirty minutes later.

The Spandex had been replaced with a pink skirt and, believe it or not, pink Mary Jane shoes. She said nothing as she led me to the small table just outside a galley kitchen. I said nothing as she set two cinnamon rolls before me and poured hot, dark coffee into ceramic mugs. She looked expectant as I took that first bite of sugar and spice and heavenly nice. "Oh my word, Sadie," I said, "men have killed for less than this."

Her face immediately dissolved into sadness. "You don't know what you just said, Mr. Whittaker."

"Call me Jake. And I'm sorry, I didn't mean to offend you."

"No, no, you said *murder* and that's what I want to talk to you about." She looked down into her coffee mug for a moment before continuing. "I saw your card down at the Laundromat. You weren't in your office yesterday, but a little girl told me you sometimes eat lunch at Frank's Bar, so I was jogged that way today."

Cora Lee. I might have known. I fingered the top of my nose, remembering how that kid suckered me into a pro bono case that almost got my nose broken. And now she was possibly involving me with a case that was about murder. No way. I don't want to deal with kids, and I don't want to deal with murder. Been there. Don't want to do it again.

While my thoughts kept me quiet, Sadie went on. "My daughter Lorna recently died," she said, "just two years after marrying a cop named Leonard Katz. She died by falling down a flight of stairs."

It was obvious she was still overcome by her daughter's death. She looked me full in the face and added, "Lorna would never admit anything was wrong, Jake, but I know Leonard abused her."

"Why do you need me, Sadie?"

"She was murdered. He murdered her. The police say Leonard had gone back into the house before she fell down those stairs, but I know that bastard husband murdered her somehow. She was ready to leave him, and he wasn't about to let that happen."

"Did you tell that to the police?"

"Of course. Repeatedly. But they've closed the case. They aren't about to believe anything against one of their own." The look of disgust on her face changed to something almost like fear. "On top of everything else," she said, "Leonard has been warning me to get off his back, 'or else,' he said."

I started to speak, but she laid a hand on my arm and leaned in closer to my face. "I'm a fighter, Jake. If I'm going to bring the bastard to justice, I need your help." She leaned back in her chair again, with her head held high. "I can afford your services." She held out a personal check and said, "This is a retainer—with a little extra." It was a pretty good-sized check.

Finding people and solving cases is what a P.I. does, but I still didn't like the word murder. However, I learned long ago you just don't say no to a grandma, especially one with money, so of course I agreed to see what I could do.

I had polished off a third sweet roll and two more cups of coffee by the time I'd asked enough questions to fill my notebook with the backstory on Lorna's death. Sadie agreed to my per diem, and even said, "Plus all expenses, including bribes."

I said, "And who the hell do you think I'll have to bribe?"

"You never know." She was quiet for a moment, and her voice became almost a whisper. "Find Lorna's killer for me, Jake."

How could I not love a grandma who enclosed her thighs in elastic and opened her mind to unrealistic possibilities? I agree to check in with her the next morning after some preliminary research. The fact that she mentioned buttermilk pancakes had nothing to do with it.

★★★

A good P.I. doesn't entirely trust the client's research. I needed background on all the prime players. I didn't have any favors to call in to get police reports, so my first stop was the home of Freddie Jacob, a fourteen-year-old computer geek who spends his summers indoors behind a computer screen while his parents are working. Don't ask me how he does what he does, I just know he can find out anything.

"No problem," Freddie said. "You want I should check both government and private records? Sometimes there's a fee or a payoff to get the info."

"Whatever it takes," I said. "I'll pay you back immediately, plus your usual overhead, of course. Can you find a way to pay up front?"

He looked up at me with a knowing smile and said, "Hey, man, there's always a way. You're asking for small stuff. I'll pay where I have to. The rest of them won't even know I've been snooping in their business."

Modern technology and young brains sure can save a lot of shoe leather.

★★★

It was early afternoon when I got back to Freddie's apartment. He had a neat pile of pages, info on every name I'd given him, plus the police reports I didn't think were possible.

"Great!" I said, as I pressed money into his hand.

Back at my office I skimmed through the paperwork before deciding I had more questions for Sadie before I headed out for some interviews.

No one answered my knock the first time. Maybe she jogged afternoons, too, but I doubted it. The P.I. in me said to try the door. The knob turned. I cracked the door open and yelled, "Sadie, are you home? It's Jake Whittaker."

Nothing. I should have shut the door and waited until the following morning, but I didn't. I opened the door and stepped into her apartment.

Her body lay on the floor in front of the couch, resting in a pool of blood that was already turning brown. Her arms were covered with black-and-blue bruises, and her throat had been cut. "Oh, Sadie!" I murmured, bending down to test her pulse even if I knew it was no use. "I'm sorry Sadie. I'm so sorry."

It was probably ten minutes before I was able to call the cops.

★★★

I didn't share my sense of loss with the cops, and I didn't share any of the info I'd gotten from Freddie either. They figured Sadie and I were friends, and I let it go at that for right then. I'd tell them about her being a client later.

I wish I could have escaped the nightmares I had that night, but I was alone with the horrors of things black-and-blue and deep pooling red.

The only hunger I felt the next morning was for the information Freddie had given me. My stomach didn't growl from hunger, it growled with a feeling of revenge. I found myself motivated to at least earn the retainer Sadie had given me.

I started by studying the paperwork Freddie had given me. Lorna's birth certificate and the marriage license for Lorna and Leonard Katz seemed legit. No surprises there. But it was another marriage license that caught my attention. Katz had been married before, and that wife had died by driving over a cliff when she was drunk. Somehow Freddie had managed to get police reports on that death, showing Katz was at a lodge meeting when someone heard the car crash at the bottom of a cliff.

I don't like coincidences. I was beginning to think Sadie knew what she was talking about when she thought Lorna was murdered by her husband. You get away with one murder, you're more likely to try another one.

Freddie's pages on Katz himself were most revealing. He was a police detective, someone familiar with the patterns of death. His service record showed two allegations of excessive force, both dismissed. I marveled that Freddie had been able to get these internal police reports.

Somewhere in the middle of reading, I knew I would continue working for Sadie. The police could do their investigation, and I'd do mine. Sadie definitely had been murdered, and if I solved her murder, I'd probably be solving Lorna's as well. Damned if I wasn't going to give it my best shot.

★★★

The police report on Lorna's death had listed a witness, but I wanted to talk to the police department before I went that route.

"Jake Whittaker," I said, standing in front of Lieutenant Cockran's desk.

It took a moment for him to put me in context before he said, "Yeah, I know who you are."

Neither one of us offered to shake hands. I was still seething from his refusal to consider murder over suicide on an earlier case I worked. He was still seething from my proving him wrong and ineffective in his job. I figured I was ahead of the game, and I intended to stay that way.

I got right to the nitty-gritty of my visit. "I understand you took over the Sadie Harrison case from Lieutenant Jackson."

"Yeah, he's got the flu." He shuffled some paper around on his desk, like I was bothering him when he had important stuff to do.

"You know I found her?"

"I know." His eyes caught mine, like he wanted me gone yet wasn't quite through with me.

"Let me catch you up, Lieutenant. Sadie was a client and a friend. She didn't deserve what she got. No one does." I gave him the information Sadie had given me about Lorna and her skuzzy husband. He knew I was talking about Katz, his fellow cop, but he said nothing.

I hated helping him with his job, but I hated Sadie's killer even more. "You find Sadie's killer," I said, "and you'll have Lorna's killer, too."

"What's with you, Whittaker? You spew so-called truth statements without a shred of evidence. You see things as you want them to be, not what they are until proved otherwise." When I didn't answer, he said, "Lorna fell down the stairs. Cut and dried. Case closed. A witness saw it happen. Sadie *was* killed, but that's nothing but a coincidence within the same family. I'm going to solve Mrs. Harrison's murder, so just back off and stay out of my way."

Now I was too mad to even acknowledge his existence. I focused on his face without looking away.

His face broke into a sneer at my silence. He looked me straight in the eyes and said, "I already have a suspect."

"And I suppose I'm it? So tell me, Cockran, what's my motive?"

This time he didn't answer me. "You tell me," he said. "Did you know the daughter Lorna?"

"I never met her, but Sadie was sure she was killed by her husband, and that's good enough for me."

"Sadie wasn't there. What Sadie thinks doesn't stack up against what the only witness says in Lorna's death."

"The witness across the street? You listened to her when she said Katz was in the bedroom when Lorna fell? I heard the witness kept a notebook about the abuse she heard Lorna was getting from her husband. Did you just dismiss the notebook?"

"The notebook didn't mean diddly-squat. The witness admitted Katz was inside when the wife fell. It's impossible he pushed her."

His eyes showed his brain was whirling. He looked up at me and said, "And how the hell do you know about Lorna Katz life, anyway?"

I just smiled at him. When I didn't say anything, he stood up as a way to dismiss me. "You'll have to excuse me," he said, "I have a real case to solve."

I left feeling angry and unsatisfied. The police would work the scene at Sadie's murder, but they weren't going to do anything more about Lorna's murder. It was up to me. I was going to revenge Sadie by somehow proving Lorna was murdered.

The itch of unanswered questions directed me to a neighborhood of well-established two-story houses where Lorna Katz had died. The Katz house was newly painted with clipped bushes on both sides of the front door. All neat and tidy. I parked out front and studied the house. There was an upper deck at one end, with iron steps and a wooden railing leading down from what was probably a master bedroom, an unusual arrangement. I cringed thinking about a fall down those stairs.

I wasn't ready to handle Katz yet, so I headed across the street for the only house that had a good view of the Katz stairs, the witness from the police report.

The door opened a crack, and a voice said, "If you're a reporter, get the hell off my property!" Jeez! The words had lashed out at me before I could even see who was talking. When the door started to close, I wedged my shoe in to keep it open.

"I have a cell phone here," she said. "Get your foot out of my door or I'm calling 9-1-1."

"Ma'am, please. I'm not a reporter." I spoke to the face peeking through the opening. "I'm Jake Whittaker, a private investigator hired by Ms. Harrison to check into her daughter's death."

The door opened to show a chunky lady with henna hair and polyester, probably about Sadie's age. "Why the hell didn't you say so," Ms. Henna said.

"I'm Mrs. Franklin," she said. Then she looked at her watch. "You're in time for a little wine. Come on in." She stepped aside to let me inside and closed the door as she headed for a credenza in the living room. "You want red or white?"

"Whatever you're having." I wanted to bawl her out for letting a stranger into the house, but instead I just accepted a glass of something bloody-looking. I took one sip and almost gagged. It was sweeter than I thought anyone could stomach.

We sat down, and she opened with, "He did murder her, you know."

"Who are you talking about, Ma'am?"

"Katz."

"But I thought . . ."

She cut me off. "Listen," she said. "I was used to hearing him yelling at her. He leaves the windows open in this hot weather, and I've heard plenty. I've called the police any number of times when I thought he was beating her, but she denied it, and the cops told me to lay off. So I started going over there and listening at the door when they had a fight." She smiled. "Those bushes by the door are pretty good cover."

I smiled at her. "Ma'am, you'd make a pretty good private eye, but I think that's a dangerous thing for you to do. Katz doesn't sound like someone to put up with anyone butting into his affairs."

Her chin jutted out. "I do what I think I should do, young man. No louse in a uniform is going to scare me."

Further warning of the danger she had put herself in wasn't going to phase her. "But why?" I said. "What did you accomplish by going over there?"

She picked up a small notebook from the coffee table and tapped it with one finger. "It accomplished a record," she said. "I have dates and conversations right here." Ah, the notebook the police report had listed.

I wanted to hug her. "Ma'am, you are a wonder and a sweetheart. Mind if I borrow your little notebook until I finish looking into Lorna's death?"

She held it out to me. "Be my guest. The cops wouldn't even read it. Said it wasn't necessary in an accident."

Suddenly I was feeling better. Maybe I'd be able to find justice for Sadie after all.

Wanting to stay on track, I said, "So what happened the night Lorna died?"

"Same ol' thing, but this time they carried it outside to that deck off their bedroom upstairs. And this time he was really yelling at her, almost like he wanted me to hear them. Lorna ran over to the stairs and was about to go down when he yelled at her again.

She motioned for me to give her back the notebook and then flipped through the pages. "Here it is," she said. " 'Don't forget your damn suitcases, you little cunt,' " she read. She turned to look at me. "I wrote it all down." She held out the notebook for me to take again.

Any gal with a notebook that looked a lot like mine was all right in my book.

"And then she fell?" I asked.

"No. She stopped at the top of the stairs while he reached inside the bedroom and shoved two suitcases at her. He said, 'Just get the hell out of here,' and then he went back into the bedroom and slammed the door. I could see the suitcases were heavy as she picked them up and started down the stairs. She took a couple of steps and suddenly stumbled. There was no way to catch herself with her hands full."

She took a large swallow of wine and added, "She made an awful noise as she bumped down those iron stairs."

"But she was definitely alone when she fell?"

"Yes, and he came out yelling her name when he heard her fall. But he didn't really care about her. Why he even stopped on the stairs to pick up one of the suitcases before he went down to where she was. Geez, she was more important than a suitcase!

"I tell you, Mr. Whittaker, if he didn't push her, he *willed* her to fall. He wanted her dead. He caused it somehow; I know he did." She gave a big sniff to add emphasis to her words, then knocked back the rest of her wine and motioned for me to do the same. I couldn't do it. My stomach would have rebelled, so I said, "I guess it's still too early in the day for me, Ma'am," handed her the glass, and said a bunch of inane things before I left.

I understood why the cops closed out the case. They were satisfied with Ms. Henna's testimony. I wasn't, not with the death of Sadie, too. How Katz killed Lorna I didn't know, but he sure as hell did it. He had to have killed Sadie too, to get her off his back.

Anger started to well up in me, and I thought I'd try to see Katz while I was there.

He was in uniform, complete with sharp pleats and sparkling shoes. His hair was on the long side of regulation, and his muscles said he probably took steroids and pumped iron. Not a guy to mess with. I poked a business card at him before he could ask. "I'm here about Sadia Harrison," I said.

"Get lost," he said. "I told Lieutenant Cockran everything about my mother-in-law, and we don't need no free lancers butting in."

"Just a couple of questions," I said. "Did Sadie have any enemies?"

"Just anyone whose life she butted into. She didn't know enough to mind her own business.

"Any particular names I should know about?"

He flexed his arm like he was lifting a weight. "Look, buddy, check with Lieutenant Cockran. Otherwise, if you don't want to find yourself arrested for impeding an on-going case, butt out. That's all I'm gonna tell you." The door slammed in my face, the conversation obviously over.

You were right, Sadie, I said to myself. He's a bastard who needs to face justice.

★★★

It was early the next morning when I headed back to Freddie's house, wanting to see him while his parents were still at work. First I stopped at the office to grab a couple of twenties I hide from myself. I needed to free Freddie's fingers on the computer keys.

I met Cora Lee just starting up the stairs to my place on my way out. She was alone except for the pile of books in her arms.

"Where's your Mama?"

"She got a new job, Jake. She started this morning as a 'ception in an account office."

"You mean a receptionist in an accounting office."

I got an exasperated look. "That's what I said. She gets to wear pretty dresses, and we'll have plenty of money for food."

"Lots of donuts, huh?"

She giggled. "Yeah, chocolate-covered." Then she remembered I was leaving. "Where you goin', Jake? Your lights were on and Mama was in a big hurry. She didn't have time to ask you nice like, so can I stay here with you, just for today? I go to Donna's tonight, and tomorrow I start day care."

Shit! I had my own living to earn. I may have been a boy scout once for a whole sixty days, but I wasn't one anymore. Except maybe for Cora Lee, I don't even *like* kids. I was going to have to talk to Loretta about this leaving the kid with me, but right now all I said was, "Look, Cora Lee, I have work I have to do." I reached in my pocket, took a key off a ring, and handed it to her. "Here," I said. "You lock yourself in the office and don't open the door or make any noise that tells anyone you're in there."

"But I thought . . ." she said.

"Well you thought wrong. Lock yourself in, you hear, and don't speak to anyone through the door or open it for anyone but me."

"You already told me that."

"So I'm telling you again."

She was pouting when I left, but I shouted over my shoulder, "Eat whatever you find up there . . . and have a good day." She didn't answer me. Good kid!

★★★

"I need background on Sadie Harrison," I told Freddie, "including organizations she belonged to, hobbies, people she hung with. You know, the works." His grin told me I was still asking for the easy stuff.

While Freddie did his thing with the computer, I hung out at Frank's place. Had one beer and two nuked hotdogs. It was a slow afternoon, so Frank had time to listen while I did all the talking. I like that about Frank.

It took me a while with Freddie when I got back. Some info asked additional questions, and I waited while he hit keys and printed what I needed.

I tested out Cora Lee when I got back to the office by knocking on the door. No sound from the other side, and the door stayed closed. "You got it right, Cora Lee," I said. "It's me, Jake. Let me in."

Such a smug look she gave me when she opened the door. I had burgers and fries in a sack, and they almost got a warmer welcome than I did. For such a little kid, her stomach turned out to be as big as mine. It was almost an hour later when I got her settled down with one of her books while I studied Sadie's life from Freddie's pages.

She'd been arrested twice, once for being part of a group surrounding an ancient tree headed for destruction and once for trying to save Native American burial grounds from becoming a golf course. She'd been married one time to the owner of a hardware store who eventually sold out to a conglomerate shortly before he died, leaving her with enough to supplement Social Security if she lived frugally. After her only child Lorna started school, she'd gone to work at the post office for a few years. Her only formal associations had been with Friends of the Library and something called Environment Now. Oh yeah, and P.T.A.

No surprises. And no help either on who might want her dead, except Katz. He wouldn't have tolerated Sadie insisting to his own police department that he, Katz, had murdered Lorna. Katz was hot headed and volatile, but it looked like he hadn't left any evidence behind at either murder. He'd done them, both of them, but so far I just couldn't imagine how with his wife.

I needed to take another look at Katz' place.

First I called the precinct and asked for Katz. "He comes on at seven," I was told. "You want to talk to Cockran?" I just hung up and asked Cora Lee what time her mother was coming to get her.

She looked up from her book. "She's done at five. She'll come get me right away."

"She better. I got places to go."

"Listen to this, Jake," she said, paying no attention to the fact that I wanted to get rid of her. "Why did the chicken cross the road?"

I knew why but didn't want to spoil her fun. "I don't know. Why?"

"To get to the other side."

I snickered for her benefit. "Dumb, but cute," I said.

For the next hour I tried to guess a zillion riddles in Cora Lee's book. It was pretty awful, but I did feel a little proud when I got two of them right.

I had a talk with Loretta when she came for Cora Lee. I finished up with, "...so never again, Loretta." I got a smile and a salute as they gathered up Cora Lee's stuff and headed out. Yes, they were still sleeping in the car, but that wasn't my problem.

★★★

Katz' house was completely dark when I parked down the block. Hoping my penlight couldn't be seen by Ms. Henna across the street, I started up the stairs at the side of the house, the stairs Lorna fell down, not sure what I was looking for. The wooden railings at both sides of the stairs were old enough to gray-out almost to the color of the iron steps. I could picture Lorna bumping her way down against the iron and wood to hit the concrete slab at the bottom.

Two steps from the top I found what I needed. Hot diggity if there wasn't a nail hole in the vertical support on either side of the step. New brown holes, not gray like the rest of the wood. *I gotcha,* my mind said to Katz.

I could picture the bastard pounding nails at each side of the wooden uprights on the railings and stringing a thin wire across the step, something that would be invisible at dusk. Katz had yelled loud enough at his wife to make sure Ms. Henna was watching from the across the street. He knew she'd see him go back in the bedroom before Lorna tripped. He knew Ms. Henna would call 9-1-1. It would only have taken him a moment to remove the wire and nails as he bent over to pick up the suitcase before going down to the broken body of his wife at the bottom of the stairs. Easy, free and clear.

But how could I prove it? As Sadie and Ms. Henna said, the bastard was going to get away with murder if I couldn't prove it. Damn!

★★★

Back at my office I popped a Coke and sat behind my desk thinking, drumming my fingers on my notebook. It was well into the night when I decided to risk my own skin to bring justice to the man I knew had killed Sadie. I would prove it through proving he killed Lorna. I was determined and scared at the same time, fight and flight all rolled into one. Plans began to circle around in my mind.

The couch felt sticky when I laid down on it and pulled up the blanket. I never should have let Cora Lee squeeze ketchup on her fries while sitting on the couch. It took a while to get to sleep.

It was mid-morning the next day before the sun managed to peek through the dirty window to shine right in my eye. I woke up aware of a fitful night filled with monsters hiding in the closets of my mind.

After a quick stop at a copy shop, I hit a deli where it took three cups of strong coffee to get my nerves jumping at the same rate as my fear. I thought I knew how Daniel felt going into the lion's den, confident but scared just the same. I was about to face Katz, not knowing if the scene would play out as I imagined.

★★★

The door to Katz' house was closed, but front windows were cranked open to let in the morning breeze. I couldn't see any movement inside.

It took him a while to answer my knock. Those on the night shift sleep during the day, and he was barefoot and wore a bathrobe. As his eyes recognized me, he grabbed the doorframe like he wished it were my neck. "Didn't I tell you to butt out of my life?" he demanded.

I swallowed and yelled back at him, "The name's Whittaker, and I think you might want to hear what I have to say."

"Not interested."

"Okay, have it your way." I turned toward the street at the same time I kept my distance from him. "Listen up," I yelled to the whole neighborhood as loud as I could, directing my words toward Ms. Henna's house. "I know how Lorna Katz was murdered!"

My eye caught his movement, and I ducked, but his hand still connected with my shirt and dragged me into the house. He slammed the door and then slammed me into a chair in the living room. My nightmare was beginning to happen. I think I was saying some kind of little kid's prayer until he stepped back and visibly tried to compose himself.

"You know nothing," he said. Then he amended it to, "There's nothing to know." With that, he did something totally unexpected: He left me sitting there and disappeared through a doorway. I could have taken off. I was scared enough to take off, but I didn't.

He returned almost immediately with two cold beers and handed me one before sitting down on the couch. We both popped the tops while trying to outstare each other. He took a swig, and I pretended to take a swig, not letting my mouth touch any part of the can. I wasn't trusting this guy with anything.

Katz ran his fingers through his hair, flexing the muscles in his arms to be sure I knew who was the alpha dog, who would be calling the moves. "My wife fell down the stairs. I was in the house," he said.

I needed to slow down the action, put a little time into the conversation. "So you say," I said.

"No, so says the old biddy across the street. She saw me go back into the house *before* Lorna fell."

"She said you and your wife were having a fight."

"Yeah, so . . . ?"

"So your wife was leaving you."

He made a noise like it was a ridiculous idea. "A temporary arrangement, a cooling off time, that's all."

"I don't think so. I think she'd finally had enough."

A fire built briefly behind his eyes. He obviously didn't like being told he didn't always have complete control in his life, but his voice remained calm. "You don't know what the hell you're talking about," he said.

"I'm talking about how you killed your wife."

This time he breathed out a raspberry sound. "You got a vivid imagination, Whittaker."

"Do I imagine the nail holes opposite each other at both ends of the second step? Do I imagine you stringing a wire between two nails there? Do I imagine you carefully planning your wife's fall after she said she was leaving you? You bet I do!"

"She said she was leaving me every day. Why would I . . . ?"

"This time you knew she meant it."

"Oh sure. I certainly must have told her, 'Wait a minute, sweetie, while I wait for you to fall down the stairs.' "

I had no good answer for that. Maybe he knew what was coming and planned ahead. I answered with, "I don't know the time frame, Katz, but maybe the neighbors know something."

This time he snorted. "You're fishing, Whittaker. This neighborhood loves having a cop living under its nose. Makes 'em feel safe. I'm telling you again, you know nothing."

"I figure the cops probably haven't seen the nail holes on the stairs, but maybe they'll be interested when I point them out."

"Two things, dick head: *One,* this is my precinct, and *two,* you're dumber than you look if you think a couple of nail holes would hold up in any court."

"How about a journal from the lady across the street?" I said. "She recorded dates, times, and events. Whole conversations between you and your wife. There are threats in there. It sets a pattern."

"You're bluffing."

I pulled out the pages Freddie had copied for me. "These are from Mrs. Franklin's notebook."

His face began to sag as he read through some of the pages, but he kept up the denial. "She couldn't know what was said in this house."

"Wrong. You leave your windows open. She came over and listened."

"It's nothing but an old biddy's imagination." With that, he tore the pages in half.

"It's only a copy," I said.

"Still worthless shit," he said, but this time he didn't sound as sure.

"All right," I said, "then let's talk about the other murder you committed."

"What the hell is that supposed to mean?"

"Sadie Harrison, that's what. What happened? Did she rag to your cop friends too much about you murdering her daughter? Did she mess around with your tidy little life which included getting rid of a wife who finally got fed up with your abuse?"

For a moment I thought he was going to throw the beer can at me, but instead he drained it and set the empty can on the table. I put mine down, too.

His voice was calm when he spoke again. "Sadie Harrison was a meddling busybody who was turning Lorna against me. I hated her, sure, but I didn't kill her."

"One of the reasons I'm here," I said, "is because I found someone who saw you going into her building just before she was killed." It was a blatant lie, but it was something Sadie's killer might believe.

"Who?" he said, making the mistake of not saying it was impossible because he wasn't there.

I just smiled. He knew I wouldn't tell him.

"You were there, Katz, and I think you warned her to back off one last time with a beating. I think she still told you to get lost, so you took a knife to her throat to shut her up."

He was back to smirking as I spelled it out. When I finished he said, "All Sadie's knives were accounted for and none had any traces of being a murder weapon. I told you, you got nothing."

I didn't like the pictures our conversation was producing in my mind. I was seeing the beaten body of Sadie lying in a pool of blood and the splashes of red fanning down one wall and on the nearby furniture. "Where are your bloody clothes, Katz? An incinerator? How about your car? Think there'll be any traces of Sadie's DNA on the seat of your car from when you drove back home? How many cases have you solved with less evidence?"

He wasn't buying it. "You're missing something, Whittaker. A yapping biddy keeping a diary isn't going to show sufficient motive. There's no murder weapon. And don't forget that a cop's word is still sterling, particularly in his own precinct." He looked so damn smug, I wanted to punch in his face.

Instead, I threw him a curve. "You carry a pocket knife?"

His hand started toward his pocket before he stopped it. He didn't need to answer my question.

"I bet no one checked your pocket knife," I added. "You know how good forensics is these days with traces of blood and pieces of skin, even if you think you cleaned a knife good. We both know, Katz, that perfect murders have a way of becoming not so perfect."

He sat there with his muscles tightening and his fists curling into balls as I came to the end of my spiel. Now his chin jutted out again. "I don't make mistakes," he said. It was almost as good as an admission.

"You call killing your wife a mistake?"

He could no longer stay calm. He stood up and yelled, "My wife was leaving me, actually leaving me! I wasn't about to lose something that belonged to me."

I stayed where I was and looked up at him. "So you rigged the stairs. When?"

He shrugged. "The day before, when I figured what she had in mind. It just took a couple of nails and some fishing line."

"What about Sadie?"

"Fucking broad was making big waves. She opened the door and let me in, so I figured she was asking for it. She deserved it."

Now I stood up and did some yelling of my own. *"Deserved to have her throat cut?"* I said.

This time the words poured out of him before he had a chance to realize what he was saying. "Yeah, she had it coming! I hit her to shut her up. She fought like hell. I had to shut her fuckin' mouth up!"

I pictured Sadie lying on the floor, surrounded by blood. Frustration and anger shoved aside my normal concern for Jake Whittaker. I yelled, "She was a woman seeking justice for her only child. You might have gotten away with killing your wife, but you're going to answer for killing Sadie."

He stood stock-still and looked at me. Then he had the gall to grin. "In for a penny, in for a dollar," he said. Then he took one step to the side so that he was between me and door. Damn, how'd I let that happen?

My need for revenge began to be overshadowed by fear, but I kept up the façade of confidence. "Oh sure," I said, "a third murder is sure to draw attention away from you. There are others who know I'm working on this case."

His grin held. "No body, no murder," he said. "I told you, I don't make mistakes."

Now I really dissolved into fear. Every nerve ending in my body called out the danger, and I felt my legs begin to jiggle. I could no longer control the look on my face. I suddenly knew exactly how Daniel felt when he faced a lion that had skipped lunch.

"Where's it all stop, Katz?" I managed, fighting for time. My script for this scene was falling apart, and there wasn't time for a rewrite. I obviously *do* make mistakes.

"Right here," he said. "I stops right here."

He was reaching in his pocket for the knife when I threw myself at him, pinning that arm in the pocket. The next few seconds were full of arms and legs and straining muscles. I kept him in a bear hug so he couldn't take a full swing at me, but he pounded on my kidney until I felt my legs start to buckle. My only advantage over his superior muscle tone was that arm trapped in his pocket.

But it wasn't a fight I was going to win.

And then, *bam,* the front window of the house shattered. Katz and I both kept our grip on each other, but we looked toward the window and saw the rock lying on the middle of the floor. Someone was out there.

There was just enough hesitation on his part for me to disentangle myself and push away from him. I got the hell out of there, but he was right behind me. I was just clearing the steps outside the door when I felt his hand grab me.

Then we both saw Mrs. Franklin in the middle of the street with another rock in her hands—and a cell phone. She was backing up toward her house, looking scared, but she stopped and held up the phone. "I heard what you said, Officer Katz," she said, "and I have it on my phone and called the cops. They should . . ." And then we all heard the siren coming down Eighty-Third Street.

Katz let go of me. He gave me a look of pure hatred, turned, and went back into his house.

The squad car was just pulling up as I put my arms around Mrs. Franklin to give her a big hug. "Sweetheart," I said, "you are one gutsy lady."

Lieutenant Cockran jumped out of the first squad car. He saw us standing there and wrinkled up his nose at me in disgust. I put an I-told-you-so smile on my face.

Mrs. Franklin looked up at me and blushed as red as her polyester pants suit. "I saw you go in there, and then I heard you two yelling. I was scared for you. I thought maybe I should listen."

"I wanted you to listen, Ms. Franklin, but I didn't want you to be in any danger. You shouldn't have thrown the rock."

"Oh yes, I should have. He was going to kill you, kill you like he killed his wife and that Sadie person you were talking about."

"I'm just glad you listened," I told her. "I hoped you would. It was the only way to nail the creep." I wasn't proud of my hoping she would be a part of my plan. I really *shouldn't* have done it. What can I say?

The uniforms were knocking on Katz' door when we all heard the shot from inside. The uniforms didn't move an inch. They knew. Mrs. Franklin looked shocked. None of us wanted to believe what our ears were telling us: The lion had eaten his gun for dinner. It wasn't the revenge I wanted for Sadie, but there it was.

I murmured soft things to Mrs. Franklin as I walked her home. Neither one of us wanted to watch while the uniforms did their thing.

Sadie, I thought to myself, you managed to bring the bastard to justice after all.

I think we both found peace.

CHAPTER 7
TIT FOR TAT

The guy hobbled into my office on crutches, the crossbar wrinkling his silk suit under the armpits. He frowned like he still felt the pain of a broken nose held in place by a wide strip of tape. I would have felt sorry for him if I didn't also sense arrogance radiating from his mangled body.

The pit of my stomach told me that if this was a client, I already didn't want the job.

He still hadn't said a word as I waved him to the chair in front of my desk. Once he was settled, I said, "I know, you ran into a door."

"I ran into the damned Cat in the Hat!"

That brought up images of a book Cora Lee read sixty-eleven times. I managed to smile instead of laughing. "It looks like you came up against both Thing One and Thing Two," I said, "but let's start at the beginning." I held out a hand across the desk. "As you could see from the name on the door, I'm Jake Whittaker, private investigator." His hand was smooth like someone who never knew physical labor but was as clammy and uncomfortable as my feelings for him.

"My name is Gregory Rockwell, the third," he said. "I'm VP in charge of credit at Tri-Cities Bank." He leaned back in the chair and waited for me to be impressed.

Geest! What the hell was a third generation snob doing in this part of town in the upstairs office of a P.I. who lives and works in the same small room? I let the lift of my eyebrows ask the obvious question.

"Two days ago," he said, "I was mugged by someone seeing through holes cut into an oversized red-and-white striped hat pulled down over his face."

"You should have let him have your wallet."

"He didn't want my wallet. He wanted my leg broken, and he threw in the broken nose before he said, 'Tit for tat,' and ran off down the alley."

"Did you give the cops a description anyway?"

"I'm not bringing the police into this. The bank can't take the publicity." He waved away the protest I was about to voice, and said, "Look, Whittaker, I want to find out who did this—or who hired it done—and I want to find out quietly."

"What're you gonna do when you find out who? Break *his* leg?"

"I'm going to see he never gets a loan anywhere in this city, and his life gets far more unpleasant than just walking around on crutches."

I didn't believe in his rationale at all. "Somehow," I said, "that just doesn't sound like a retaliation that would bother your Cat in the Hat—or probably his Keeper. Besides, I don't deal in revenge."

"Do you deal in justice? Do you deal with stopping this creep from doing it to someone else?" He sneered, either at the so-called creep or at me for not jumping on his revenge bandwagon.

It took a lot of talking on my part to get him to agree to only filing a complaint if and when I found the guys—which I had little chance of doing in the first place, and I didn't believe him in the second place. But in the third place, I could use the hourly rate I'd be paid. An evangelist would be proud of my spiel to him that fell just short of forgiving seven times seven. It's one of the things my Granny spouted to me as a kid when Randy Matlock keep beating me up. But most of what I said went over his head.

He did agree to documenting his injuries with written words, pictures, and after-the-fact witnesses. I agreed to take the case because the retainer he offered was almost double my usual per diem plus expenses, including three meals a day. It was probably my visions of prime rib and filet mignon that made me ignore I was about to delve into investigating violence. You might say I was willing to overlook the sleaziness of this sleaze ball when I had dollar signs in my eyes. Or maybe I just didn't like the Cat in the Hat being used by the seamy side of life. Surely Cora Lee and her Mama would never condone anything to do with violence either.

★★★

Before he left, Rockwell handed me wad of bills and a list of people who had recently been denied loans by his bank, plus a list of his possible personal enemies, who included three ex-wives and an ex-partner of a financial firm that had gone belly-up before he hooked up at the bank.

Shit, I doubted if even the guy's bartender liked him.

But my bartender Frank loved me when I paid my line of credit in full. In turn, I only ate half a bowl of pretzels when I got the free beer Frank often gives whenever I catch up on my bar tab. I sat on my bar stool with visions of possibilities as the beer slid down my throat. When I left there, I headed across town to the home of Rockwell's latest ex-wife. I figured the other two ex's were probably past anger and well into thankfulness that he was out of their lives.

The house was less pretentious than I figured a silk suit would have left behind in a divorce settlement. But the woman who opened the door would have upstaged a Barbie doll. She was the stereotype trophy wife who is eventually replaced by a newer version.

She frowned when she saw me and quickly hooked the screen door. I tried to ignore the insult.

"Mrs. Rockwell?" I said.

"I'm Ms. Hennessy now."

"Sorry. I'm Jake Whittaker, Ms. Hennessy. I'm investigating a mugging your ex-husband suffered that was probably intentional."

That turned her frown into a wide smile. "You don't say," she said. "Who do I congratulate?"

I ignored that and handed her my business card. "Can I come in, or do you want to talk here?"

She looked down at my card, but she didn't back up one inch. "Here's fine. What do you need from me? I'm not the one who roughed Gregory up but I certainly had reason to."

"Reason?"

She looked at my card again and said, "Look, Mr. P.I., I'd have to stand in line to wish the creep ill will. He's a cheap bastard who goes out of his way to avoid a good deed. If he had children, they'd disinherit *him*. If he's found a new wife — his *fourth*, by the way, she better be good with makeup that covers bruises. And if he sits across from you in a business deal, watch your back." She bored a hole through me with her eyes before adding, "Anyone who knew him might just want to 'work him over.' Is that what you want to know?"

Before I could answer she stepped back and slammed the door, leaving me shaking my head to throw off the venom she's spewed out, her own kind of revenge against Rockwell. I wasn't going to get anything more out of her this trip.

I headed for Antonio's Restaurant. I didn't like my client, and I didn't like working for him — much as I was probably going to fail. But I did like Antonio's medium-well steak with all the trimmings.

★★★

The next morning, after a skimpy breakfast of a caramel donut, I went to the office of Rockwell's ex-partner. It was an upstairs suite of two rooms in a building that actually had an elevator. There was the requisite blonde behind a computer in the outer room who took my business card, read it, and then looked up at me. She said, "Do you have an appointment?"

I looked her right in the eye and said a simple but emphatic, "No."

Her shoulders gave a small shrug as she turned to a phone and turned her back on me to try to speak so I couldn't hear. I couldn't. She hung up and waved me toward a chair as though I knew I would have to wait. I sat. I waited.

I looked around. A saw the gold lettering above the reception desk that said John Candlemeyer, Financial Advisor. Underneath, in small letters, it said And Accounting Services. Well, well. But evidentially Mr. Candlemeyer let oak furniture, discrete paintings, and a compact table with cups and a coffee maker talk about his success. It was an okay attempt as a confidential business.

I heard a small beep, and the receptionist pointed to the only door in the room that wouldn't take you back outside and said, "Mr. Candlemeyer will see you now."

The man behind the oak desk smiled, offered me a hand, and said, "I understand you're a private investigator." His smile got bigger, and he said, "Don't tell me, your business has gotten too big for you to handle the bookwork yourself."

Don't I wish! "No," I said, "I'm investigating the intentional mugging of Gregory Rockwell."

His smile disappeared in a flash. "Oh really! Well, can't say I'm sorry about that. First of all, Rockwell stiffed our growing financial firm, and then he stiffed me personally by expensing out the profits before the partnership dissolved, leaving me high and dry! Second of all, even if I hated the guy — and I do — I'm not about to want to be anywhere near him."

When I didn't say anything, he added, "Don't look at me as the one who hurt the son of a bitch, but you find the guy and I'll pay his legal expenses."

Like the ex-wife, Candlemeyer didn't know of anyone who *wouldn't* want to beat Rockwell up. He grabbed a piece of paper, though, and wrote a couple of names he thought I might want to check out. Then I got a definite dismissal smile and left.

He never did ask me to sit down.

★★★

Back on the street I leaned against a wall and looked at the names and references he had provided. One jumped out at me. Suzanna Galetti was one of Rockwell's ex-girlfriends, but she could be related to Johnny Galetti, owner of Exotic-Erotic Restaurant and a fringe member of organized corruption in our fair city.

I found a phone and looked up the address of the ex-girlfriend, then headed into the hills where the real money lives and plays.

★★★

It was Little Bo Peep who answered the door, complete with crooked staff and a fluffy shirt just long enough to cover the essentials. I was too startled to say anything and just let my eyes talk for a moment. This shepherdess didn't have Galetti's rough looks at all; she had the beautiful body and face of someone who could tend my sheep anytime.

"Oh," she said, "I thought you were Joseph."

"I could change my name," I offered. She smiled and then read the business card I handed her.

"So, Mr. Whittaker, what's a private eye like you want with an actress like me?"

I smiled back at her. "Oh, so you're an actress. Children's theater?"

"Sure, that'll do." She let her smirk tell me what neither one of us was going to call a spade a spade. I've been around the block, as they say. I've known specialists in all fields, and if Bo Peep had a specialty, it wasn't with wooly sheep.

"I'd like to talk to you about Gregory Rockwell," I said. "Can I come in?"

The crooked staff clanged down on the tile floor as she pulled back from the door. Her eyes shifted up and down the street as though I might be a front for someone else more sinister. "What the hell is Gregory trying this time?" she said, more in fear than in anger.

"Whoa, I'm not going to harm you. I'm trying to get a fix on who might have roughed up Mr. Rockwell."

"Well, well, can't say I'm surprised. My only question is why someone didn't give him his comeuppance sooner."

"My question," I said, "is why this guy is on everyone's shit list."

"That's easy. He wants what he wants, when he wants it. His way or no way. A self-centered control freak. He screws everyone within screwing distance. Anyone and everyone could have wanted to get back at him."

Before I could come back with another question, a guy scurried up the walk behind me.

"Joseph!" Miss Bo Peep said. Then she murmured at me, "Make an appointment." As I started to walk off, I heard her say, "Pesky salesman!" before she let Joseph into the house and closed the door.

★★★

Frank's bar seemed the logical place to go next. I wondered if I could call that an expense on a busy detecting day. I'd have to have Frank write me a receipt.

When I tell my bartender everything, I know he won't repeat it. Frank seldom speaks one word that isn't absolutely necessary. He listened to my rundown on this latest case and shook a finger of understanding at me when I repeated Bo Beep's and Candlemeyer's call on Gregory Rockwell and the Cat in the Hat mugger. I got a small smirk out of Frank when I rounded out the picture with the ex-wife's venom.

I thought out loud and said, "I know, I know, I probably gotta check out every one on every list to find the one person who wanted to give Rockwell as good as he gave." Frank just raised his eyebrows. The wheels in my head were oiled with beer. I almost wanted to solve the *who* by copping to it myself!

Ignoring my tab this time, I slapped a ten on the bar and left before Frank could draw me another cold one. I was headed for Johnny Galetti's place, but not before my expense account tallied up a steak sandwich with two sides at Kiki's Kitchen. Mid-afternoon was the earliest Galetti would show up at his restaurant anyway.

★★★

The heads of exotic animals still stared at me from the walls of Exotic-Erotic. I kept my eyes on the erotic waitresses instead of the animal heads as I passed through the dining room to the offices down a back hallway. This time I didn't bother knocking before opening the door marked "No Admittance," but this time I didn't find Galetti making whoopee with his latest chippy. He sat alone with his feet on the desk and a phone to his ear. "Look," he said, "you either get with the program or suit up for war!" Then he slammed the phone down and glared at me.

"What the hell do you want, Whittaker? I told you I didn't want to see your face in my place ever again." He was oozing sleaze that brought bile to my throat. Still, I tried to play it cool. "Ahhh," I said, "it sure is hard to miss me if I just won't go away, huh?"

"Maybe it's your turn to suit up for war," he said.

"You might get a little over-extended," I answered. "You already have your troops fighting at the Rockwell front."

An eyebrow went up, and he answered with a sneer. "Who's Rockwell?"

I didn't acknowledge his question. "Rough stuff is right up your alley."

"I'm not into rough stuff."

"Did I say rough stuff? I meant intimidation like you just laid on the poor smuck on the other end of the phone."

"It was just an idle threat."

"I'm not buying it. I don't know what Rockwell did to you, but I think you just answered my question on who arranged for Rockwell to get a dose of his own medicine — and we both know why. Testosterone wants to take care of things for little sisters, don't you think?"

He didn't say anything. Now that the Cat behind the Cat in the Hat's mastermind was out of the bag, we both knew where I was heading. I continued with, "Look, Galetti, I don't figure you ever read a book in your whole life, but I'll keep to the script anyway. You are about to come up against Thing One and Thing Two." He looked at me like I was talking crazy, but I just continued with, "Thing One is you laying off Rockwell from here on in. I'm betting he's already making the connection on *why* .he's got pain, and he's got enough money to back retribution if he finds out the *who*. Thing Two is that *who* will be our little secret if you cease and desist."

The line of his mouth told me he was already agreeing with both Things, but I could also see future crutches under my armpits just because of my one-upmanship. I had to think fast.

"In this case," I said, "there happens to be a Thing Three. If you're unhappy with me, you have a 50-50 chance of getting me, but I promise you a 90 percent probability it'll backfire. But who knows, maybe you'll like prison. I cover my back and I'll cover your bet on yourself for whatever it's worth — or have a big bother with law enforcement."

He didn't bat an eye. He just said, "Get the hell out of my office, Whittaker, keep your yap shut, and don't ever, ever come back here again!"

I let my body show confidence I didn't really feel, giving him what I hoped was a Clint Eastwood glare before I walked out. It wasn't until I'd closed the door behind me that I slumped against the wall for a moment. My heart needed to get off the treadmill before I could walk back to my car.

★★★

My gut feeling told me to get all my expenses from Rockwell before I made my report the next morning in my office. I spent a couple of hours attaching receipts to my expense report, and then tackled the close-out report for Rockwell.

In the morning he glanced quickly at the bottom line of the expense report and shelled big bills out of his wallet before settling back and listening to the web of deceit I wove out of whole cloth. I let them lay there on my desk.

"What do you mean it was a jealous boyfriend!" he screamed. "What boyfriend? Who's boyfriend?"

"I'm talking about a guy who thinks Ms. Suzanne Galetti is exclusively his, and he treats her like a princess and anyone else around her like a knave. I'm guessing you may be one of those who sniffed around her. You've felt the results of how he thinks."

He bit his lower lip as anger started to bubble up on his face. "What's his name?" he demanded.

"Oh for crying out loud, Rockwell, cut your losses. Is a pretty face worth getting the other leg broken? Is your little black book so empty you have to risk life and limb for someone you can find in any singles bar—for the price of a steak dinner?"

His eyes showed the wheels turning in his head, but it took a while before he came around to agreeing with me. Finally he said, "I want his name! You're getting paid to give me his name!"

"Then it looks like I'm not getting paid."

He stared at the money on my desk, considering if he wanted to take them back. His face turned hard as we sat opposite each other with a standoff neither of us was willing to resolve. Without another word, he stood up, ignored the money on the desk, shoved his wallet into his back pocket as a statement, and stomped out of my office.

It wasn't the first time I had to settle for my "up front" and expense money without anything further, but the "up front" had been pretty good. And my expenses, more than slightly padded, made it worthwhile. The prime rib at Delmonico's last night was still making happy sounds in my stomach. Maybe I'd go back again tonight.

Life is that way sometimes for a P.I.

CHAPTER 8
STAKEOUT

It was a feet-on-the-desk kind of day that called for a nap. A voice jarred me awake just as a spot of drool hit my Hawaiian shirt. "Do you remember me, Mr. Whittaker?" the voice said.

When my eyes began to focus, I recognized Pat Gnomes, the poetry editor from Plebeian Publishing, the one who first voiced the clue to solve the case. This was also the person whose looks, clothes, or voice didn't give a clue to being either a man or a woman.

I rubbed my eyes and motioned at the client chair. "Of course I remember you," I said. "And you can call me Jake." With a professional look pasted on my face, I added, "I'm not sure how you found me, but I'll just accept it. How can I help you?"

"Are your investigations always private?"

"That's what the sign on the door says."

"Good. I want to know who's blackmailing me."

"What do you plan to do if and when I find this blackmailer?"

"You get right to the point, don't you?" I could see the wheels turning in Gnomes' head. "I'm not planning on committing a felony. Maybe just a Mexican standoff."

"I suppose you aren't going to tell me the theme of this blackmail."

A smile appeared across from me. "Of course not. Let's just say it's about my private life."

A homosexual? A bisexual? *A sex change?*

"How does he, or she, manage to put the screws on without your knowing who's doing it?"

"I got a letter I won't show you. You'll have to take my word for it. To arrive no later than today I'm to mail $5,000 cash to a box at a mail service called The Mail Tub. I want you to find out who picks up the envelope."

"You're going to pay it?"

Gnomes shrugged. "Until I know who it is, I don't have a choice."

I sighed inwardly. Stakeouts weren't my favorite activity. If I'm going to sit still that long without going to sleep, I'd rather it were on a barstool at Frank's where the beer is cold and the pretzels salty. But what the hell, there was always too much month left at the end of my money. I needed the work.

Gnomes agreed to my per diem plus expenses, and I agreed to watch Box 162 at The Mail Tub. We both agreed to meet the following evening after I'd run the stakeout.

On the way out, Gnomes' husky voice said, "I mailed the money yesterday. You just need to find out who picks it up and be sure not to let the blackmailer know I'm looking for him."

"You know it's a 'him'?"

"No, it could be a she. Just find out, will you, whoever it is."

I couldn't stop my eyes from following that ass as it headed out the door. Damn, was I lusting after a man or a woman? Maybe only the blackmailer knew for sure.

★★★

I'd called The Mail Tub to check out their hours and when mail was distributed. We were talking about a neighborhood where any business, even a mail service, didn't dare leave its doors open at night. At least I'd be able to sleep on my own office couch. I'd never stay awake on an all-nighter.

By the time The Mail Tub opened, I was parked outside with a scratch sheet, a capped bottle to pee in, two containers of coffee, and a dozen donuts from Ferguson's bakery. My rusty Chevy already had a half sandwich from yesterday and several chocolate bars.

I rummage under debris in the back seat for my binoculars and tested my view of Box 162 through the plate glass window. Perfect.

I was working on the third race when a short little fat guy with a long, stained apron walked toward Box 161. I brushed the powdered sugar off the binocular lens in time to see him reach out to open a box, but damn if his back didn't block my view of which box. He ended up with some letters and a large, fatty envelope, but I couldn't see the box number. I'd have to find out which box he'd opened the old-fashioned way: I'd have to earn it.

I was out of the car by the time he hit the sidewalk. "Excuse me," I said. "Can you tell me how this mail service works? I'm afraid they won't give me the true scoop inside."

He gave me a look usually reserved for annoying children. "You pay for your box, and you get your mail. What'd ya expect?"

"Is it private, really private?" I waved at the boxes inside. "Do *they* know who you are?"

He shrugged and grinned. "Not if you give 'em a phony name and address." He leaned in toward me. "You got a frigid wife who works in your butcher shop like me? Well, she knows how to use sharp knives. She don't need to know you got a little sexy side business that brings in money she don't need to know about. Know what I mean?"

"Hey, brother, that's exactly what I mean!" We swapped macho smiles while I hoped my face didn't show disgust for whatever type of porn he was into.

"But how are letters addressed? Can you show me?"

He backed off and jerked his pile of letters behind his back. "What the hell you trying to pull? You see return addresses, and I end up in jail. You perverts got no scruples at all." His face turned as red as the stains on his apron. He said, "Get lost before I show you how little blood means to me."

It was too early in the day to bleed. I backed off as he folded his arms in front of him in anger, but now I could see the top letter in his hand. It was Box 1-6-something, but his thumb covered the rest of the number. Shit, I'd had better luck with liar's dice at Frank's Place.

He stalked off in a righteous rage as I climbed back into the Chevy to write the bloody butcher in my pocket notebook. It looked like I might have to check out meat markets if I didn't get lucky with someone else by the end of the day. With the deadline Pat had been given, I was almost certain the perp would show up this first day after the hush money was mailed.

I was rubbing my eyes to keep them open when damn if Ferguson from the bakery didn't show up and head toward the area of Box 162. I shot out of my car and stood against the edge of The Mail Tub's window like I might be waiting for a bus, even though the bus stop was two blocks down. My slanted view would keep anyone from blocking my line-of-sight. But hot damn if he didn't lean his right hand against some of the boxes as he opened a box with his left hand, blocking my view. Again. Then he stepped back and shuffled through his mail. Pulling out a yellow card, he went up to a counter at the far end of the building and handed the card to a clerk.

I caught him as he came out with a couple of packages. "Well, Ferguson," I said, "I see we have more in common than donuts."

Recognition hit him at the same time as the flush on his face. "Oh, Whittaker, yeah right." He straightened up and pointed toward The Mail Tub, trying to regain his composure as he clipped out words. "Packages. Bakery supplies. Quick.

Easy." He shifted the packages so they were under the other mail he was carrying.

Good golly, Miss Molly, what cheap ingredients was he using in his bread dough? *In his donuts!* My stomach turned, trying to rid itself of the donuts I'd packed into it. Now I'd have to find another bakery, not easy in the district where I had my office.

Or maybe Ferguson's story about bakery supplies was just a cover-up for a blackmail business. One of the packages in his fist was fat enough to hold $5,000 cash.

I winked and said, "Yeah, same here. The Mail Tub is an easy way to keep my secretary from thinking I can afford to give her a raise. She doesn't need to see all my mail."

A secretary? I had to do my own hunt-and-peck on my old Olivetti. I lived in my office with the bathroom down the hall. A secretary? It almost made myself laugh out loud.

Ferguson stopped looking uncomfortable. It was good-old-boys time for him. "Right," he said. "What we know and others don't know can be a real boost up the financial ladder."

Alleluia! The words of a true blackmailer. I love it when this job is so easy.

"Color me rotten but color me rich," I offered.

"You got it! And who knows the difference anyway?"

Now I was confused. Maybe I was right the first time. Damn. I hate it when I'm right and then decide I'm wrong instead. But something definitely was not right about Ferguson.

I mumbled something at him as he turned away, then I went back to my car. I added him to my notebook, still needing to know if he adulterated his baked good—or if he was collecting blackmail.

My eyes were stinging with the need for sleep by the time a third man hovered in the area of Box 162. I eased out of the car to watch a guy with thick glasses and blackened fingers start to reach out for a box. But he stopped and started looking around like an actor in a 40s spy film. When he saw me through the window, he backed away from the boxes.

I tried to blend into the bricks surrounding the window, but he wasn't buying it. He hesitated for a moment, not making eye contact, and leafed through some brochures sitting on a counter. I walked inside like I was a box holder.

He went up to a woman behind the counter, flipped his wallet open to show who he was, and obviously began asking her into giving him mail from his box. This one wasn't going to be easy.

He was finally handed a pile of mail and headed for the door. I managed to catch him just outside the building. The mail in his arms didn't readily show any addresses, but I caught the title of a magazine called *Coin Collectors*.

"Excuse me," I said. He stopped. I pointed to his magazine and said, "I see you're a coin collector, too. You buy and sell them also?"

"Coins. Metals. I'm a metalsmith." The lopsided look on his face said something more.

"Interesting. What kind of things do you make?"

That opened him up. I could see he liked talking about his work.

"I fashion some pretty good candlesticks in pewter or silver," he said. "Not a real popular item these days of TV trays, but I do okay with them. I also make zodiac key chains, decorative bowls, and tourist souvenirs. It's a living."

"It doesn't sound very lucrative."

He scrambled to sound successful. "Anything pays if you know how to play it. There are people out there who'll pay a fortune to add to their collection."

A candlestick collection? I don't think so.

He was on a roll now, proud of his business savvy. He grinned again and added, "Metal can turn into money more ways than one.

Counterfeiting? No one bothers to counterfeit coins . . . unless it's counterfeit collectors' coins.

"Right," I said.

His smile told me the conversation was over, and he walked off down the street.

Back at my car, I was left wondering why he was renting a box from The Mail Tub when Uncle Sam delivers for free. I doubted he was Pat's blackmailer, but I was sure he was running some kind of scam. What's wrong with the people in our world? I sighed. Ah well, at least the world's scum kept me in business.

The only other person who went near Box 162 for the rest of the day was a gray-haired old lady who opened Box 159. I amused myself wondering if granny had a secret lover — or worked for an escort service for seniors. At least the speculation kept me awake.

When The Mail Tub closed for the day, I had an hour to kill before meeting Pat Gnomes. I headed for Frank's bar to nurse a beer and flush the donuts out of my system, hoping sawdust and beer don't solidify. I sat on my usual bar stool and thought of the meager data in my notebook. The way I figured it, Gnomes' blackmailer had to be one of the three men I'd seen that day, but I didn't know which one, and I couldn't prove it if I did. I'd have to tell Pat that my investigation now had to go beyond The Mail Tub.

★★★

It was a different Pat Gnomes who bounced into my office and sat down. The doubled-breasted jacket and sensible shoes still didn't give away gender, but the twinkling eyes tried to tell their own story. "I won't need you any longer," Gnomes said.

"Why? You know who the blackmailer is?"

"No, but I don't need to know. After I paid the price, I realized I was never going to be free and have any peace until I risked being the one to open up my private life."

"And?"

"And I did. It's great! A total relief."

I cocked one eyebrow with a question I couldn't quite voice.

"Hell no, I'm not going to tell you. I'm not an exhibitionist."

I chuckled. "Okay, but let me report on my day so you'll know where your money went and who to cross off your Christmas list."

I let Gromes know that I had three suspects and began giving a rundown, telling how I had been planning to follow up on each of them regardless of any blackmail.

When I told about the metalsmith, we both agreed he was in some sort of metal swindle but probably wasn't the blackmailer.

When I explained about Ferguson the baker, Pat yelled, "Oh yuck, that's where I buy my bread!"

"But does he know about your private life?"

"No. Oh wait a minute, there was that time I left my private mail on the counter in his shop. Maybe . . . no, I don't think there was anything special in my mail that day. I'm not sure, but I don't think it's him."

"My guess is that Ferguson's too busy with adulterating baked goods to jump into a sideline of blackmail."

"Was there anyone else?" Pat asked.

I started telling about the butcher but got interrupted. "Wait a minute," Grimes said, "is he short and heavy-set?"

"Yeah. You know him?"

"I've met him a couple of times at Petersen's. He's Casey Baxter who owns a shop on Sixteenth. Says he makes his own sausages. Don't tell me he puts . . ."

"I don't know, but you might want to find a new butcher, too. I think he's into smut of some kind, and I don't mean just humorous limericks. Maybe videos. Maybe prostitution. Anything ring a bell?"

Gnomes shrugged and ignored my question, but I could see I'd hit pay dirt. "It really makes no difference, Jake. You found three scoundrels, but I no longer care who was blackmailing me. I consider the money I gave the scrum and the money you earned well spent. It's over and forgotten."

"I don't like to leave things unfinished," I said. "I'd like to do something about people running illegal scams that hurt other people. Okay with you if I turn in my suspicions to the proper authorities? There'd be no mention about any blackmail."

"Be my guest."

I rallied to the thought. "I know a certain lieutenant down at the precinct I might be able to appease after some past bad feeling between us. He might be interested in a porn broker or a coin fabricator. Only the Health Department will be interested in questionable bread ingredients. I'll let them run with the three rat-finks. My mother always said there's a time when bad actions catch up to us."

"Go ahead," Gnomes said, getting into the swing of things. "Maybe the police can catch my blackmailer at *something* and maybe catch a couple of other scumbags to boot." With a smirk, Gnomes added, "What would your mother say to that?"

Memories flooded into my mind. I voiced my answer to Pat in words almost like those I'd heard from Mom:

"Jake," she had said, "never do anything that you don't want anyone to know about—unless it's giving to charity." I wasn't much into charity, but I did have some things in my past . . . I chuckled to myself with memories.

Cora Lee would have giggled and said, "That's silly, Jake!"

CHAPTER 9
NO TIME OFF

It was a Sunday afternoon when Frank brought my first beer of the day. He leaned toward me and actually started to say something when a customer at the other end of the bar yelled for service. Frank put up a finger to tell me he'd be back to continue a conversation we weren't even having. I was surprised. For a bartender he doesn't talk much and acknowledges customer stories and tribulations with only raised eyebrows and lopsided grins. If the adversity is really bad, he might come back with a single word like, "Bummer."

He didn't get back to me until I signaled for another beer. As he set it down, he threw a short letter in front of me.

"What's this?" I said.

He just pointed for me to read it. It was a copy of an e-mail from someone who signed herself "Kitty." It explained how she wouldn't meet with Frank until she had sent someone to check him out. I looked up at him. "You're surfing the web for dates?" He shrugged.

"Well, whoever checks you out is gonna know you deal in alcohol, but so what? You've got the license and the rest of us have the thirst. It's an honest living." I thought about that for a moment and added, "You did tell her you own a bar, didn't you?"

He nodded his head but still said nothing and waited for me to push it further. "What?" I said. "You afraid Kitty's gonna find out something bad about you? That you print bogus bills in the back room?" I got a dirty look, so I got a little more serious. "Maybe all the receipts don't go in the register for the IRS tally?" This time he just wagged his head, so I said, "Okay, Frank, I've been in here enough to know you're not loan sharking, making book, or running numbers. I always wondered why not, but that's another story. What are you worried about?"

"Who?" he offered. His head nodded toward the other end of the bar like he thought Kitty had sent one of his present customers to check him out.

"What makes you think it's someone who's here now?"

He threw another paper in front of me. This one was dated yesterday. "Hey, Frankie," it read, "if Sunday is a slow day, maybe that's when I'll send a crony to check you out. Keep an eye open."

My eyes shifted up to Frank's face. "She calls you Frankie? That's real sweet . . ., Frankie!"

He didn't acknowledge my question, but he did blush slightly. "Find out," he said. Wow, two words. We were having a real conversation, even if I wasn't sure what he meant. Fishing a cat out of a toilet is more fun than getting Frank to open up. Did he want me to find Kitty's snoop?

"You want me to use my vast, incredible powers as a P.I. to find out if Kitty sent someone who's sitting at the bar right now?" This time he nodded, and I even got a half smile.

"Okay, how about a swap? I find this person and you erase a part of my bar tab. In reply he put his finger up again, thinking it over. "Naw," I said, "this one's on the house from me to you. Okay?"

His head bobbed up and down a couple of times. "Okay," he said, and then he was gone, checking other glasses, questioning about needed refills with the lift of an eyebrow.

Well damn, I thought. I come in here to get away from work, and my very own bartender puts my shoulder to the wheel.

I sighed and looked down the bar to see what I was getting into. There were three guys and one woman at the bar, and there were two tables with women, one with men. The easiest ones to approach were the loners who were bellied up to the bar.

Mr. Suit-and-Tie two stools down looked like a good place to start. His clothes spoke attorney or salesman and he was well on his way to getting drunk. But this was a Sunday, not an attorney or salesman day. So he was probably a preacher after a hectic church service, or possibly someone scared about meeting a blind date. As I fished around in my mind for an opening ploy to approach him, I absently flicked at puddles of foam on the bar in front of me, making matching stains on both sides of my shirt. Finally I decided to go with my best impression of Mr. Suit-and-Tie, slid my glass down next to his, and plunked down on the stool beside him.

"I've got a question," I said.

"I didn't come in here to talk."

"You do enough talking in the pulpit, right?"

That got his attention. He took on a surprised look and said, "Yeah, so?"

Bingo! Either I was better at this P.I. stuff than my wallet showed, or he thought he'd go along with whatever I said. Keeping reproach out of my voice, I said, "My question is how come one of you born-again types is in a bar?"

The stumbling in his mind showed up in his words. "Well ... if you must know, I ... I'm working on my future."

Hot diggity, that was a new one. I managed to not laugh, but one foot started jiggling in mirth. My feet don't have the same control I do. "How's that?" I managed to ask.

His shoulders slumped like he needed to get something out. "Mrs. Digby and Mr. Matthews," he said.

"What about 'em?"

"Three weeks ago Digby was saved. She was so drunk she almost couldn't make the altar call."

"Did it take?"

"Damn right it did!" He fingered a couple of bills lying next to his drink. "When she came back sober the following two weeks and testified how God has saved her from alcohol and how thankful she was, the collection basket was piled high with big bills. Everyone figured God had healed her."

"And Mr. Matthews?"

"Same thing. He swore off liquor, stayed off, and the basket gobbles up paper every time he testifies. A bonanza."

"So what's wrong? Didn't you get credit for Mr. Matthews?"

"Hell no. God got the credit."

"Bummer," I said. "But what's that got to do with your future?"

He took a swallow from his glass before he answered. "Ah . . . there's another church service tonight. If I show up drunk and then come off the booze, I can testify *every* friggin' week. Can't always depend on Digby and Matthews to fill the basket. I testify week after week, the whole church gives week after week. Simple as that That basket holds my future."

"Hey, you're selling us drinkers short. It takes more than one day to become a drunk. Anyone can repent after a one-day binge."

He thought about it for a moment. "Maybe I can say I've been a closet drinker," he reasoned, "until tonight when I walk into evening services drunk. If it worked for Digby and Matthews, it should work for me. God will see that I repent. Besides, I need this boost in my belief." I think he meant a boost to his wallet.

My other foot began to jiggle with mirth. I loved it. This guy had rationalization down pat. I probably looked a little skeptical when I said, "So you believe God is going to come through for you? You believe that?"

He said, "My cup will runneth over. God wants me to be rich. I'll see it and *then* I'll believe it."

I started sliding my beer back to where I had been sitting before and left him by saying, "Maybe you'll see it *when* you believe it."

Frank ambled over like a dork at a debutante party. "Definitely not him," I said.

"Try again," Frank mumbled.

"Hell, Frank, they're all gonna think I'm soliciting if I go from guy to guy." He managed to shrug and plead at the same time.

I sighed and resigned myself to fate.

Trying to be systematic, I eyed the next guy down the bar. Checkered shirt. No shit, it looked like he was wearing a tablecloth from an Italian restaurant, probably his idea of casual. Jogger shoes. He didn't fit Frank's usual red neck customer, those who would take offense at supposed same-sex solicitation. A guy can get hurt badly with such a misunderstanding.

To play it safe, I left my glass and passed by Checkered Shirt on my way to the loo. On the way back I stopped and pointed at his shoes. Determined to "just do it." I said. "Nike?"

He held a foot out and said, "Forget about shoes with those fancy names. Forget uppers and linings. It's the sole that counts." He patted the sole of one shoe like I should be impressed.

"What are you talking about?"

"These are Treadwell Soles. You tell me what the foot's gonna do, and I'll show you the perfect sole."

Eeesh! a salesman. I never met a salesman I liked. But I needed to know if he was just putting me on, so I plunked down next to him and said the magic words any salesman wants to hear. "Tell me about them." I braced one arm on the bar, pasted a smile of interest on my face, and tried to tune out my brain.

For the next ten minutes I found out more about shoe soles than anyone ever wanted to know. Just coming from the bathroom, I couldn't even escape by pleading I needed to take a leak. Somehow I unshackled my ear from his mouth and let my boredom limp back to my stool. When Frank ambled over again, I just whispered, "Those are the soles that try men's time."

He didn't understand me, of course, so I added, "It's not him." This time I was the one who shrugged. "This is useless," I said.

Frank whisked away the flat beer I had been too bored to drink and set a new cool one in front of me. Call it a payment or call it a bribe, he wanted me to continue. In spite of my limit, I took a sip, checking out the only other two people sitting at the bar, a man and a woman. I crossed the man off my mental list right away. If he was there to check out Frank, there was no way he'd remember anything tomorrow. He had trouble finding his mouth with his glass of wine, his spine had trouble staying vertical, and his clothes needed to be introduced to a washing machine. I could almost feel the headache he was going to have the next morning.

That left the upsweep hairdo at the far end of the bar. She didn't have the hard look of a woman who frequents bars. She had a pleasant face and the slightly pudgy look of someone you might want to cuddle in different surroundings. The glass in front of her looked like tomato juice with a celery stick, definitely not a usual bar drink. I didn't know Frank even had celery sticks.

I figured her for the lonely, bored housewife whose husband spends his Sundays golfing, bowling or watching TV sports. Or she could be sitting there doing her friend Kitty a favor. I was about to find out.

"Do you happen to know anything about celery?" I asked when she looked up and saw me standing beside her.

She gave me one of those looks and said, "That's an original line."

"Well, what can I do when I live alone, have finished the Sunday paper, and really wish I had a dog to talk to?"

Her quirky smile showed her humor. "So maybe," she said, "you go to a bar to find a dog?"

My face flushed hot as one hand clamped itself over my stupid mouth. "Oh no, I didn't . . . not for one minute . . . never . . . I didn't mean it that way at all!" I stammered.

Now she was laughing out loud as my brain went into overload, but there was kindness in the crinkles around her eyes that gave me the courage to speak again. "Maybe we'd better start over," I said, holding out a hand. "I'm Jake Whittaker."

Her grip was firm. "Catherine,," she said. "What brings you here besides celery?"

I pointed to the other end of the bar. "I own that stool down there, but can I sit here for a moment?"

She waved a hand at the empty stool on the other side of her, inviting me to sit. Without a single word, Frank brought my glass down and left us alone.

"You obviously aren't a bar girl," I said. "What brought *you* here if it isn't celery?"

She churned her drink with the celery as she thought how to answer. "I'm trying to figure out how to appear happy and successful."

"A divorce?" I asked. She nodded. I mentally patted myself on the back. Either I was psychic or a whiz-bang at this P.I. stuff. "They do say happiness is the best revenge, but you won't find success in here." Then I smiled at her. "A puppy dog, on the other hand, will always think you're a success. And it's cheaper in the long run."

"Money's no problem. My ex's secret little mutiny with the local butcher's wife translated into alimony for me."

I nodded and agreed. "Ah, I see. Alimony is the bounty after the mutiny."

She giggled. "Very funny! But it's true." Her head wagged. "I'm getting on with my life. Maybe I should date the butcher."

My stomach suddenly did a little belch, throwing out warning signals. "Wait a minute," I said, "I hope you're not talking about the butcher on Seventeenth. Between Oxford and Argyle? The short, fat guy?"

"Yeah, it was his wife my ex was seeing. Probably still is. Why, what do you know about him?"

"Holy shit . . . oh, sorry, Ma'am. Stay away from the butcher and his wife. I think he's into porn, and he's not the forgiving type when someone messes with him. He has sharp knives and has said, 'Blood means very little to me.' "

Her face paled. "Good grief, is George in deep trouble, running around with the butcher's wife? Should I warn him?"

"Just don't date the butcher."

"I was only saying that. I already have someone else in mind."

I was so intent on her situation that I didn't even realize what I was saying next, but I couldn't have made a better choice. "Well, check him out first."

"Don't worry, I am."

Jackpot! Even I could see I was coming up smelling like roses. This dog's day had come. My chickens were hatched and could be counted. My number was a winner. Now it was time to earn my payback for Frank.

"Too bad," I said, pointing to Frank, "otherwise I'd introduce you to Frank. He's available and would be the perfect, successful revenge for a two-timing ex."

"How's that?"

"He owns this place." I swept a hand around the room, taking in the bar and the small tables crowded against the opposite wall. "After five o'clock on a weekday there isn't an empty seat in here, and Frank could get carpal tunnel pulling beers for thirsty workers. He probably has a bank account with more zeros than the old Japanese air force."

"Yeah, but what is Frank himself like?"

Here's where I could really earn my P.I. status. There's a fine line between lying and laying it on thick, and I managed to accomplish both. "He's trustworthy, loyal, helpful, friendly, courteous, kind . . ."

Her eyebrows raised in protest.

"Okay," I said, "he was probably a good Boy Scout in his youth. He doesn't talk much, but somehow you know there're layers down there just looking for a pogo stick to spring out words." I wasn't very good at this touchy/feely stuff like women like, and I wasn't making much sense, but she seemed to buy it.

"You make him sound like a real paragon."

"Take it from me, he is."

Then I did the only thing I could do. I waved Frank over. I pointed to Catherine and said, "Frank, I want you to meet Catherine. I think her friends call her Kitty. Kitty, you're gonna like Frank."

With that, I got up and walked toward the door, leaving my beer behind. Work is definitely the curse of the drinking men.

CHAPTER 10
NOT A GOOD PICK

Damn, damn, damn! I was leaving the racetrack where the ponies had left me with only twenty-two dollars when someone in the thick crowd almost knocked me over, kicking my shinbone in the process. Damn it hurt! The clumsy oaf gave me a sheepish look, mumbled regrets, and got out of my way. It was all I could do to limp to my car, and suffer my way back to my office/home where I could sit behind my desk and finger the knot on my shin.

The pain was down to a small ache when the door to my office opened and a scruffy specimen silently walked toward me. Without a word, he threw a wallet on my desk. Damn again, it was *my* wallet! My hand automatically patted my empty back pocket as reality dawned on me. This was the cretin who had bumped me as I was leaving the track.

I came up out of my chair with my fists raised.

"Hear me out!" the cretin said.

One of my hands turned into a pointer at my wallet. "Nothing you can say is gonna cover a sore leg and a flat wallet."

"Your money's still there. All twenty-two bucks."

I checked. It was, along with some of my Jake Whittaker, P.I. business cards. I scooped the wallet into a desk drawer, reminding myself how stupid I'd been to carry it in a back pocket in a crowded place. But curiosity also pecked at me. My finger shifted toward the client chair. "Sit down and tell me why I shouldn't call the cops," I said.

His palms went up in the air as he sat down. "Look," he said, "I'll give it to you straight, and then if you want to call the cops . . . I'll just have to fade outta here."

He admitted he was a pickpocket "by trade." He unsuccessfully tried to rally sympathy by saying he only operated at places where people were going to go home broke anyway: the track, bars, sporting events, and expensive restaurants. "But," he said, throwing another wallet on my desk, "yesterday I also came up with this."

I didn't touch it, not in these days of fingerprints. Instead I raised one eyebrow and waited. With a shrug he picked up the wallet and slipped a torn piece of newsprint out of it. "Inside I found this," he said. Opening it, he placed it in front of me. Words from a marker were written across two newspaper articles:

FIRST AND MAIN   10:00 TOMORROW
AND IT BETTER LOOK LIKE AN ACCIDENT

Oh boy!

All sorts of scenarios ran through my head. But there were just as many questions. "Whose wallet?" I said.

"Some schnook named John Deerfield of Atlanta, Georgia, of all places. No money, just pictures of his family.

"You try checking him out?"

"Hey, I just got the damn thing today. You're the private eye, you check it out."

I let all that go for now. "What makes you think the 'tomorrow' in the note hasn't already passed," I said.

"I bought today's paper. The articles the note is written on were there."

"You taking this to the police?"

"Hell no! My record with them is very minor and ancient. As a picker I don't have a record at all. I'm that good. I'm not about to let them know I exist, let alone how I earn my three squares."

"Earn?"

He had the decency to look sheepish.

"Okay," I said, "what's your take on this?"

"Sounds like a hit to me. The time and place are there, but we're missing the name of the victim and how it's gonna happen."

I thought about it. "Maybe . . ." I began. "Try this out for size. Maybe some guy's going to have an arranged first meeting with a girl, without her knowing about it."

"You really think that?"

I looked at the note again. "It's probably just something I wish was true." I had lots of questions. "Think ten-o'clock is morning or night?"

He shrugged. "How the hell should I know? All I know is that I want to hire you to be at First and Main tomorrow to stop whatever is gonna go down. I don't want this on my conscience."

"You have a very selective conscience," I said, but I was already figuring the per diem the cretin would bare. I knew exactly where I'd be at ten o'clock tomorrow morning, and again at night if necessary.

He agreed to an hourly rate with an advance that probably came from the wallet of another sucker with a sore shin, and I agreed to attempt to try to stop an undefined crime. But the hefty advance he gave me would be satisfactory even if he didn't come back late the following night as promised.

He took the note and the other wallet when he left.

★★★

Cora Lee and Loretta had found an efficiency place over a produce store where Loretta worked a second job helping display veggies that arrived early each day. Then she dropped Cora Lee at Day Care before going to her job at the accounting office. Saturdays Loretta liked to goof off, so I took Cora Lee to an early movie at the Tenplex downtown, a block off First and Main. It was one of those cartoon shows where the kids enjoy the animation and the adults enjoy the subtle word jokes done with familiar voices. Afterwards, we went for ice cream while I listened to Cora Lee's complete replay of the entire movie. If there's a sequel, I'll feel like I've already seen it.

"Feel like a walk?" I finally said. I winked at her and added, "Let's walk over to First Street. I need to 'case the joint' before tomorrow."

"Sometimes you talk so silly, Jake."

"You're the one who told me silly is good."

She wiped off her mouth and got up. "What are we *casing*?" she said.

"Let's just say I want to see if it's a safe corner for kids."

First and Main is a pretty busy intersection, even in the early evening. There are traffic lights and left-hand turn lanes. There are walk lights for pedestrians. Mom-and-Pop stores are open to foot traffic at ten in the morning but closed by ten at night. Most of the night foot traffic was from the local movie theater or restaurants. There were apartments or lofts above most of the stores.

Everything seemed normal, no way for un-accidental accident to happen. I even looked up to see if a flowerpot might find its way off a roof onto a head below. I didn't expect to see anything threatening, and I didn't.

"Is this a safe place?" Cora Lee asked.

"Hey, kid, when you're with me, I'm always gonna keep you safe." She gave me a quick hug, which made sitting through a silly movie suddenly okay. By the time I got Cora Lee home, she was asleep on her feet. Loretta helped her stumble inside, and I went to Frank's bar to figure possibilities.

I ate a whole bowl of pretzels while I nursed a beer and thought about how someone might kill or hurt someone on an open street and make it look like an accident. A drive-by shooting? Risky at ten o'clock in the morning, but it might work at night. Push someone in front of a fast-moving car? That had potential. A mugging at night might also work, assuming it came under the category of a random act and hence an accident.

I voted for pushing someone into traffic.

But I'd have to pick a potential victim *and* perp out of all the people at First and Main at whichever time of day it would happen. And I'd have to split my personality to be on all four corners at once. The writer of the note could bring the unsuspecting victim downtown for a movie and ice cream like I did Cora Lee. Something could happen to someone who opened a shop alone at ten in the morning. It could even happen to someone who would "fall" from an upstairs apartment. I hadn't thought of that possibility earlier.

My head whirled. I signaled for my second beer, realizing how hopeless it was to anticipate a crime with so little information. I ran all the scenarios past Frank and watched him shrug and nod, occasionally responding with the single word, "Bummer." I left there feeling frustrated, but at least someone else knew how hopeless this case was.

I didn't sleep well that night.

★★★

I was downtown at nine in the morning, milling around, watching cars, looking up at rooftops, seeing how people waited together for a walk light before crossing the street. Of course, if something went down in the middle of the block, I wasn't going to see it from the corner, but life is like that. As ten o'clock moved closer, I was antsy and just wanted to go home, but instead I started watching body language and where other people were looking. I told myself a Secret Service agent couldn't have done a better job.

There were two guys who seemed to be headed nowhere, hanging out, looking in store windows, waiting. When they turned toward the street, their eyes searched the crowds, maybe looking for the victim, or maybe innocently waiting for a cohort to show up for a nearby meeting. I kept a low profile and watched both of them. It was ten twenty-five when I figured neither one of them was going to do anything drastic, so I gave up and went back to my office.

I felt like a failure, but there was still ten o'clock that evening.

The rest of the day I piddled around with paperwork and did something I seldom do in the middle of the day. I took a nap on purpose instead of falling asleep from boredom. Stakeouts are particularly boring. This time I was stuck with nerves that had been on alert too long, and the uncertainty of not knowing what the hell I was doing on this case in the first place. Finally I decided to just forget about the whole case. It wasn't my problem.

You know, though, where I was at nine thirty that night.

I ran through the same litany of observations, this time straining to see things with only street light illumination. I crossed the street in every direction enough times to stake out squatters rights. And I saw two more guys milling around and keeping an eye on the crowd. One could be the one who wrote the note, and the other could be the, what would you call him, the "hit man?" Or was one of them the victim? Hell, I never felt so lost. Again I wanted to go home, but of course my legs refused to leave the corner. They always did have a mind of their own.

As ten o'clock approached, my nerves were on standby. Since I couldn't be on all four corners at once, I was ready to shout out whatever I could to stop something bad happening on one of the other corners.

I had glanced at my watch one more time when I suddenly saw a man put his hand under the arm of the woman next to him while they were waiting for the walk light. They were almost in front of me, one step away from cars whizzing past them. His grip tightened on her arm, and my muscles tightened in anticipation. When I thought he made a move forward, taking her with him, I bumped against her, throwing her back and almost throwing myself into the traffic in the process.

"What the hell!" the guy said, as they both stepped back.

"Be careful!" she said to me. "You'll get yourself killed if you don't wait for the walk signal." She had a hold on my arm, pulling me back toward the sidewalk. She must have thought I was rushing the light.

The guy wasn't buying it though. Both of his fists balled up. "Either you're an idiot who needs a Boy Scout, or you're a pervert. Move off or you'll regret it." Everyone stood there and watched the three of us, not even crossing the street when they could as the walk light gave permission.

"Come on, Daniel," the woman said to her companion. "We still have the light."

Jeez, it was embarrassing as hell. If I ever felt smaller, I didn't know when.

I was still mumbling apologies to two people who were no longer there when the walk light again gave permission to cross the street. People left me alone there at the curb.

And then I felt myself being grabbed by the shirt from behind. When I twisted around, I was staring into the face of one of the two guys who had been surveying the street that morning. The other one was crossing the street toward us.

"Well, well, well," Shirt Holder said. "Looks like we got ourselves the perp."

The other guy gave me a knowing grin and said, "Sure looks like it."

"I was trying to save a life!" I said.

Both of them broke into laughter. "Sure you were," Street Crosser said as he took a flat, leather folder out of his pocket and presented a police badge in front of my face. The next thing I knew, I was spread-legged against the bricks of the nearest building, patted down, and cuffed. "Your picking days are over," Street Crosser said.

I was mortified. "Picking?" I said. "What's that got to do with making something look like an accident?"

I was being pushed into a squad car as Shirt Holder said, "You're a good pickpocket, pal. You managed to elude all attempts to get a handle on who you are. But this little sting of ours is gonna take you down."

Okay, you don't have to hit me with a two-by-four to have me see the whole picture. The handcuffs were enough to let me know I had been had. There was a double con here, and I was the sucker. The cretin had finally picked the wrong pocket, and he had enough of a conscience to fall for a planted note. He was smart enough and weak enough to find a chump to do his legwork. The cops had been watching for the pickpocket as I watched for some hit man who didn't exist.

The P.I. had finally turned into the victim. It wasn't a day that was going to go into my memoirs.

There was laughter when I showed by at the precinct in handcuffs. The biggest laugh was when we passed by Lieutenant Cockran's desk.

During the three hours I was in the station, I had to endure several rather improper remarks, but I gave back almost as good as I got. They did listen to me when I told them to preserve any prints that might be on my wallet. "And be careful not to add your own prints, you bastards," I said. "I wouldn't want to have to pick any of you out of a lineup." I put on a good show, but it was touch-and-go there for a while. I had to field questions and felt like the fool I was when I gave my answers. I gave them a description of the real pickpocket and even sat with an artist until he'd sketched a good likeness. Ah, what the hell, the coffee was strong, even if they didn't have any donuts.

It was a long, tiring day. I knew I was stiffed out of my per diem, but I had the hefty advance to soothe my bruised ego. And I didn't have to write one of those damned client reports.

CHAPTER 11
ART WORK

They may call us gumshoes because we P.I.s put in a lot of walking, but hiking to an auto supply store was not on my wish list that day. The weather was foul, and my shitty mood matched it. Being cold was the only reason I stepped into the art gallery on the way to get a new fuel pump.

People with turtlenecks and long skirts were setting up a spread of food and wine at a long, central table. That table definitely had potential for a cold, hungry gumshoe hiker. I eyed the food but ignored the people as I stepped over to the closest painting, a seascape by the featured artist, a woman named Dahlia Duncan. I hoped no one could tell I was rubbing my hands together from the cold rather than from admiration of the paintings. I don't give a hoot about art.

Evidentially Ms. Duncan had over-stocked on blue paint, because every single one of her paintings was of the ocean. Why? We didn't even live on the coast.

I pretended interest as I stepped from picture to picture, waiting and hoping to hear the pop of a wine cork that would signal the food was fair game. If I played this right, I could nibble my way through a free meal before finishing my trek to the auto supply store. My rent was due again, and I was already making meals from pretzel bowls at Frank's bar where my tab was again quickly approaching overload.

With my eyes on one of the paintings, I bumped into a table full of self-help books. A man was arranging them in piles. It was Josh Phelps from the publishing company where I'd recently investigated an employee who was taking more than his share of the profits.

I called out his name and held out a hand.

It took him a moment to connect my face with a name, but he came back with, "You're Jake Whittaker, aren't you, the private eye snoop who fingered Kevin Beals?" I was surprised he remembered, but he jumped in with, "And you have a good memory for names, too. You must have read my book, *Magic Memory Minders*."

I couldn't help but chuckle. I pointed to the books. "How come self-help books are at an art opening?"

He picked one up from the table and held it in front of my face. *Paint It, and They'll Buy It.*

"So?"

He waved a hand at the paintings on the walls before tapping a finger on the book. "Dahlia Duncan read my book and is now a successful artist." He pointed to a woman across the room and said, "That's her there." Duncan was a willowy woman of about thirty-five, dressed like a successful gypsy. She was all proud smiles as a patron gestured toward one of her paintings.

"My book got her started," Phelps said proudly, "telling her to paint what people want and to stick with it." He rolled his eyes and looked down at the floor. "Frankly," he said, "Little Miss Dahlia was a mediocre artist before she read my book." It was an attempt at being humble that missed its mark.

"So why is she letting you sell your books here? I would have thought it was her night to shine."

He shrugged and looked up at me. "Damned if I know. She called and made the offer, said she was going to give me some credit for her success. It'll sell books, so I wasn't about to refuse." He was quiet for a moment before he added, "We used to be an item, but somehow I think she's just using me again."

While I mulled that over, his face turned serious. He leaned in close to me for a moment and whispered, "Something's going on with her and her paintings, and I'd really like some answers. She couldn't have gotten that good after just reading my book, sorry to say. I think I need your P.I. help in figuring it out, Mr. Whittaker. Are you expensive?"

"Not cheap, but reasonable."

He laid one hand on the book table. "Will you take a retainer in books?"

"Hardly. Why, what do you need me to do?"

"Follow Dahlia. She has a studio she holds strictly off limits. She wouldn't even let me see it when we were going together. I need you to watch her at work so you can tell me how the hell she does what she does. Frankly, I don't think the talent is there." His hand circled out to the paintings and then to his book. "And yet . . ." he said. "So I'd like to hire you to find out how she does it. Somehow I just need to know."

I started to object, but he cut in with, "I know, I know. Look, I want to find out how she got successful. I want to know what her studio is like and if she actually does the paintings herself. For all I know, she has a six-year-old nephew who paints what he saw at the seashore."

"Why do you care? You said she learned from your book."

"Frankly, the book's not that good, not good enough for her to go from mediocre to great almost overnight. She got successful about the same time she gave me the heave-ho. I want to know what happened."

I made no promises, but he agreed to pay my per diem, whether I was successful or not. I took three twenties as a retainer and at the last minute grabbed a copy of *Big Appetite, Small Budget* as a bonus.

Although the art exhibit hadn't actually started, people were beginning to filter into the gallery. I took the opportunity to snatch several cheese cubes and some crackers off a table no one was guarding.

Then it was back outside to get the fuel pump. I dreaded installing it myself, but I had no choice.

★★★

The cheese and crackers had to suffice for dinner. Once the car was working again, I drove back to the gallery just before it closed. Back inside, I munched my way through the leftovers, ignoring the little mushrooms with who-know-what stuffed inside. The wine was gone. Damn.

As Dahlia Duncan was saying her goodbyes to the gallery owner, I went outside. When she came out she looked exhausted. Her auburn hair frizzed out wildly around her face, detracting from eyes that seemed to promise things you knew she'd never delivery. She now had the hard look to someone who's been there and is not about to go again. I like 'em soft and cuddly. She had a hard, calculating look.

I followed her car several miles out of town to a lonely rural house surrounded by an uncluttered lawn and trees around the perimeter. I parked under a tree just off the road and watched Duncan leave her car in the driveway. It didn't look like she locked it. Ah, the country life where things are simpler.

There was nothing more I could do that night, so I shifted into drive and headed for Frank's bar to shuffle my thoughts by passing them through Frank's non-verbal mind. I had the questions, but he was smart enough to not offer any answers. He never does, he just listens. After one beer I put a twenty down on the counter, said, "Off my account," and took off for home.

★★★

It was going on noon when I dragged myself off the office couch. Hearing my mother's voice in my head, I dutifully folded the blanket and stashed it under the pillow at one end. I needed coffee, and my stomach was beginning to demand food. Hunks of cheese on silly little crackers hadn't stuck with me.

I was thinking bacon and eggs until I located a three-day-old bagel in a crumpled deli bag. It was a challenge for the teeth, and the little seeds on top looked rather like something a rodent left behind, but it soothed the growling in my stomach.

There was almost a bounce to my walk when I took the stairs to the street level and tried to remember where I'd parked the car the night before. I found it covering half a red zone painted on the curb. I figured the fact that there wasn't a ticket on the windshield as a good omen for the rest of the day.

I picked up carry-out coffee on my way back to Duncan's house, sipping it slowly while running schemes through my mind that might get me invited into her artist studio. It wouldn't be easy because I don't know one damn thing about art. I don't even know what art I like when I see it.

"Good afternoon," I said when she answered the door. "My name is Jake Whittaker. I was at your opening last night."

"Yes?"

"Your wonderful paintings made me wish there was an ocean around here. I can't believe how well you paint the sea and the waves and . . . well, you know, those little flying birds. There is such power in your work."

She wasn't quite buying it. "I'm not in the phone book," she said. "How'd you find out where I live?"

She got my biggest smile. "Reporters never tell their sources."

She held the door between the two of us, like I might kick it in. "You're a reporter?"

"Would you like to see my business card?" I said, reaching toward my pocket.

"No, that's okay."

I didn't even have to pretend I'd just run out of them. The pretense of honesty almost always beats the real thing.

I pulled out a pencil and my pocket notebook. "I'm sorry, I should have told you right away. I'm with *Mixed Media* magazine. We're doing a series on newly-successful artists. We'd like to include you as a segment for our October issue." I let her think about that while I tried to look sheepish. "I wonder if you could possibly give me an interview."

She still wasn't buying it quite yet, but she didn't say anything for the moment.

"Wouldn't you like to see your name and talent in our magazine?" I said. "Could I come in and talk to you about it?"

Her face told me she was becoming convinced, vain enough to overlook her reservations. She stepped back and opened the door for me. Hot diggity, in like Flynn! Only Flynn never had the finesse of a Jake Whittaker.

When she led us into the living room, I said, "If it's okay with you, I'd like to interview you in your studio, maybe watch you paint. You know, get the full ambience of the artist in her work environment. Then of course I'll send our photographer to get pictures for the article." It sounded good to me.

A frown crossed her face, and she hesitated before she spoke. "I seldom let anyone into my studio," she said, "but if you'll stay here while I tidy it up a wee bit, then I guess I could show you around. But you can't watch me paint." I started to protest, but she added, "It's the only way if you want me in your magazine."

I managed to shrug and smile at the same time and waited until she was gone before I snooped around. A large office room was connected to the living room through a wide archway. It was full of computer equipment, an oversized printer of some kind, two bulky copy machines, and a large light table. I recognized what they were, but being able to use anything electric or electronic is almost as foreign to me as artwork. I can't even use the "self help" machines at Kinkos.

I was back in the living room by the time she came to lead me to a large room at the back of the house. A full wall of bare patio doors brought in sunlight to shine on two easels facing the windows, holding two in-process paintings of the ocean that I pretended to admire.

"How do you make it look like the fog is hanging over the sand here?" I said.

"Layering."

"And how do you make the sand look wet where the waves are coming in?"

"Ah that," she said. "I mix a secret ingredient in with a darker color . . ." Her voice trailed off like I was asking for a prize family recipe she wasn't about to give up.

I scribbled words in my pocket notebook as she continued talking about her work. She gestured while talking about the techniques of one painting—supposing I knew what the hell she was talking about—and her hand brushed again a piece of clear tape hanging from the top of one canvas. She pulled it off, balled it between her fingers, and let the wad fall to the floor. That was the first thing I liked about her; she had the good sense to not be bothered by a little debris.

We went back to the living room while I got some background on her. She'd been employed as a computer programmer and dabbled in painting on the weekends. Then she read Phelps' book *Paint It, and They'll Buy*. After that, painting became more than a hobby, and she'd made the decision to leave her stressful job to incorporate Phelps' lessons into a new lifestyle.

It was too pat, too simplistic. Somewhere in her words was a truth that was hiding an untruth. There were times she avoided looked at me, and I knew it was more than the fact that I might have forgotten to comb my hair that morning.

Finally she said she needed to get back to her painting.

"Can't I please stay and watch you work?"

"Sorry," she said, "I always work alone."

"I'll be quiet as a little mouse. Just think of me as an adoring groupie."

She did chuckle at the thought, but she said, "I'm really sorry. Painting alone is a rule I *never* break."

There was no choice but to leave. I told her the magazine would make an appointment for her to be photographed at a later date, and we left it at that.

On the way back to the city, my judgment argued with my feelings. Last night I had thought Phelps was sending me on a wild-goose chase, but now I was feeling what he felt. Curiosity reared its head in my mind. Something wasn't quite right with Ms. Duncan, and I was at least earning money to find out what.

★★★

Cora Lee needed to return some library books after school that day, and I was headed there anyway. If I was honest with myself, I really wanted to put in a little research time to justify stretching a one-day job into two days in order to satisfy my wallet.

The reference librarian remembered me from last time. She sighed with resignation that she was again stuck with someone who knew so little about libraries, but she was a librarian, after all, and she led me to books on art techniques. I spent much of the afternoon looking at pretty pictures and studying drawing and painting, trying to stuff enough knowledge into my head to sound plausible as an art reporter. I even used my notebook so the right side of my brain could try out a couple of the drawing exercises I found in one book.

Cora Lee was off in the kids' room, doing her thing with books. She came and peered over my shoulder a couple of times, but I pleaded I needed more busy time, and she accepted that. Once I was busy with a nap, and she woke me up. It was annoying and welcome at the same time. I just smiled a "thanks" at her.

"You like paintings, Jake?" she said as we waited in line for her to check out her books so I could take her back home.

"Good grief, no. What makes you think that?"

"Why would you look at art books if you don't like paintings?"

Smart-ass kid. I'm not used to explaining myself to anyone, let alone a kid who had the annoying habit of talking in questions. So I asked a question of my own. "So, Missy, why do you like books on horses if you don't have a horse?" She looked up at me and laughed. "Gotcha, huh?" I said, before adding, "Sometimes adults do stuff, that's all." She accepted that, partly because it was her turn to check out her books. I hoped that put an end to this conversation, but in the car I found out it hadn't. I had to live through an explanation of why she checked out every book in her lap: horses, monsters, kids on impossible adventures. Wish I could have such enthusiasm. We headed back to her place.

I had mixed feelings as I waited at the curb until Cora Lee got inside and I could head home. A smart, inquisitive kid with a donut addiction and a love for books can drive a laid-back P.I. up the wall. Somehow, though, I didn't really care.

That night I saw bright colors in a weird dream that reminded me of a child's drawing. Yellow dripped from a round sun onto a boxy house, giving a Picasso-like image. I saw stick people of blue and orange and purple who were shorter than the grass, but at least the grass had the decency to be green. There was a square on the center of my dream picture, full of splotches of blue. Maybe it was the start of an ocean painting.

When I woke up, I was having dream jitters, so I dressed quickly, locked my office door behind me, and headed toward a café that lets me run a tab. I added a sugar and coffee buzz to my dream jitters, along with a greasy burger and fries. Cora Lee would've been proud.

★★★

It was the earliest part of the afternoon when I headed back to Duncan's house, hoping I could watch her through the windows. Her car was there, so I parked out of sight and found my binoculars on the floor in back of the car.

Staying behind the perimeter of trees, hoping I was too far way to be seen, I worked my way to the back of the house. I found a good perch and brought the binoculars up to my eyes. A new canvas was set up on one easel, but Duncan was nowhere in sight. I needed to get a handle on where she was, so I moved to the other side of the house, watching for some form of movement inside. She was in her office, her fingers working the computer keys. A few seconds later she walked over to one of the other machines and stood in front of it, waiting. Finally she pulled up a large sheet of paper, turned off the light, and went toward the back of the house where her studio is.

I worked my way back through the row of trees to get a good view of the studio. Here the natural afternoon sun dripped light into the room just like in my dream. There were no curtains at all in that room, so I had a good look with the binoculars. The easel faced the light, giving me a dandy view of the blank canvas. I watched as Duncan located a tape dispenser and taped the sheet of paper on the canvas.

Eureka! That's when I realized what she was doing. The paper was a full-color picture of the ocean with a piece of sandy beach, front and center. From that point on, I could have written the script for what she'd do next. She slid a big piece of carbon paper behind the paper ocean scene and taped that in place, too. She pulled a pointed stick out of a jar full of brushes and, oh yeah, she traced every little detail of that picture onto the canvas. Hot damn, the composition of her paintings came from someone else even if the paint came from her brushes. I figure it might not be illegal, but it had to be unethical. Either way, it wasn't my problem. Ethics never are big concerns in the P.I. business.

My report to Josh Phelps should make him happy about paying my two-day fee.

Patting myself on the back made me a little careless as I walked from tree to tree back toward my car. I didn't think about the sun and shadows.

And I didn't hear the patio door open.

"Who's there?" an angry voice said. I stopped dead still behind a thick oak. "I know someone's out there," the voice said again. It was definitely Duncan talking, a woman too angry to be frightened. "Your shadow moved across my canvas," she said. "Who the hell are you, and what do you want?"

I dared one peek from behind the tree. She stood in the doorway searching for any movement. I didn't dare move again until I saw the glint of sun on a gun she held in her hand. My head pulled back just as the noise of a shot registered in my ears. Damned if she hadn't fired at a tree about ten yards from where I stood!

That did it. Now an adrenalin rush joined my earlier dream jitters and coffee-and-sugar buzz. I was wired beyond belief. How could something as relatively innocent as the art world turn into a life-threatening situation? Guns scare the hell out of me.

Shit, I should have been an accountant!

I didn't dare move and show myself. She was trying to scare anyone who might be outside her house, and it was working. Not one muscle in my body dared to move, and I was profoundly thankful there were no more shots. Neither did she come out with her gun to investigate. Whew!

Finally the patio door whooshed closed, and I dared to peer around the tree again. Taking one last glance out the window, she went back to her canvas. Maybe she just thought her imagination was working overtime. And then again, maybe I only had eight lives left.

I took a deep breath and got the hell out of there.

★★★

"I need proof," Phelps said.

What for? I told you she's tracing pictures she got off the computer. You said it's not illegal. You said your book suggests copying established artists as a way of gaining expertise. What's the problem?"

"The reasons are mine. The problem is I need proof."

There was no way I was going after proof. Just the announcement of a gun is enough to make my knees shake. I shook my head, letting him know it was his problem and I wasn't interested in making it mine.

"I'll pay you through the end of the week, eight hours a day" he offered, "even if you get the proof in one day." When he could see I was ready to take the bait, he added, "Proof or no proof, same deal. Just try, okay?"

Hmmm. I started weighing fear against necessity. It was a necessity that I pay rent or else be reduced to sleeping in doorways. It was a necessity that my stomach take on fuel at least twice a day. And then there was my tab at Frank's bar where it's a necessity that I pay it down periodically.

"I'll try," I finally said, knowing I would dearly regret it

He smiled as we shook hands, and he left me sitting in my desk chair wondering why I chose greed over fear.

The way I figured it, there was only one chance of getting proof without the possibility of facing a gun. One phone call told me that garbage pickup for Dahlia Duncan's area was scheduled for the following day.

Timing allowed me to spend the rest of the afternoon on another case, following a dry cleaner's wife as she took her usual day off from the cleaning business. At least that day she wasn't having an affair like her husband suspected. And at least I could swap my P.I. work for dry cleaning services. My one non-washable suit would be happy, if I ever found an occasion to wear it.

And I was happy because I was getting paid by Phelps while I was working another case. An honest double dipping

★★★

It was just turning light the following day when I drove back to Duncan's house. There was her garbage, sitting at the curb, waiting for pickup like a hooker on Twenty-Eighth Street.

And there I was, about to earn a day's fee by picking through garbage. At such times I'm sure I should have been an accountant.

Thankfully, Duncan was a faithful recycler with separate bins of newspapers, bottles, and cans. A large plastic can with a snap-on lid held what might be called "wet" garbage, the stuff coming from a kitchen where there's no disposal, along with anything else that isn't paper, tin, or glass. For a moment I was afraid she might have a paper shredder and any hope or finding proof would be in strips too small to be reassembled. I lucked out on that one. No bag of paper shreds.

What would she do with the pictures she got off the Internet after she'd traced them? I couldn't imagine her saving them; she was too savvy for that. My eyes fell on the neatly stacked newspapers in a low tub.

Was it possible? I began searching through the newspaper stack. Eureka! Folded neatly inside one thick section of newspaper was a colorful paper scene of the ocean. I dug down a little farther and found another printout near the bottom of the pile, another ocean scene in full color.

Paydirt! A full week's pay for one day of work.

★★★

Phelps looked happy when I said I'd been successful. He handed over a whole week's pay without a single question.

"This one is an 'I gotcha!' " Phelps said, holding up one of the computer pictures. "Its exact image is hanging in the gallery right now." Then he held up the other one, the one she had probably been tracing when she threatened me with a gun. "And this one," he said, thumping his finger against the paper, "I can show her when she brings her rendition in for sale. She's going to be sorry she shoved me aside."

My stomach began to feel a little queasy. For my own sake I needed some answers. "Why?" I said. "Why do you care? She read your book and is a successful artist, regardless of whose ideas the paintings are. Why not just let it go?"

His face turned dark. "Let it go?" he said. "She's the one who left me. I really loved her, and she just walked off when she didn't need me anymore. And she thinks she can throw me a bone by letting me sell a couple of volumes at her la-de-da artist shindig. Well, she better think again."

"Come on, Phelps, don't be a jackass. It's not worth it."

He hardly heard me. His voice volume rose with his anger. He pounded a fist against one of the ocean scene printouts before he folded it up again. "I could expose her as a fraud in a split second with one of these. See how she likes being hurt."

"I wouldn't . . ." I began, but his anger wasn't listening.

"Damn Dahlia Duncan!" He spewed out.

I held out my hand and said, "Let me show you something on those printouts." Once they were in my hands, I folded them up and said, "Do you know what your next book should be about, Phelps?"

He obviously didn't understand where I was headed. "What?" he said.

"About forgiving and forgetting," I said. We stared at each other until I began backing away from him, hanging onto the printouts. Finally I turned around and walked toward the door of my own office on my way out, leaving him behind in the client chair.

"She has a gun, you know," I called back over my shoulder. "She shot at me, so she certainly isn't afraid to use it."

When he held his ground and didn't come after me, I figured him for more of a coward than I am. Or maybe my words got through to him, but I doubt it. I didn't look back.

I would come back later to lock up after Phelps was gone, but meanwhile I took off for Frank's place.

Maybe being a P.I. *is* better than being an accountant.

CHAPTER 12
SQUARE ONE

"Jaaakie?" a soft, feminine voice said.
I couldn't see who was standing behind the door to my office/residence, but my heart began to flutter. I wasn't sure my mind was ready for this, but ready or not, the door was slowly opening.

"Are you available?" the voice said, this time in a teasing tone.

I answered in a voice that showed a flippancy I didn't feel. "Sweetheart," I said, "if that's you, get in here and find out!"

Yes, it was her. It was Melissa Allgood who pushed the door open and walked back into my life. I hadn't seen her since I figured out who let her partridge named Patty out of the house and where it could be found. I had wanted to call her hundreds of times, but I knew words would fail me as soon as she said "hello." That's what was happening to me now. Realizing it was Melissa for sure, no more words volunteered to come out of my mouth.

But there she was, a vision with a face that still couldn't decide whether to be angelic or devilish. I think devilish was winning this time as she wiggled that heavenly body across the office, her 1000-watt smile bringing sunshine to a dreary fall day in the life of Jake Whittaker, P.I.

I stood up and offered her a professional hand, but she leaned across the desk and gave me a quick hug. I was transported to heaven and fell back into my chair, full of hope. She sat down and crossed her legs. My day was made.

I cleared my throat and said, "How's Patty?"

Melissa twisted her fingers in her lap. "She's gone, Jake."

"She go back to the pear tree?"

"No," she said. "Patty went to bird heaven, but I don't want to talk about it." I murmured words of sympathy before she continued on. "That isn't what I came to see you about. This time I need you to find Mally."

I grinned at her. "Mally's your new bird?"

That got a smile out of her. "No, Mally's my new boyfriend."

My smile disappeared, along with a whole lot of my hope. My manly confidence was shaken. I sighed. "Okay, tell me about it."

She said she hadn't known Mally long, but she assured me they were in love. It figured, Melissa doesn't do things halfway. They'd met when Melissa was feeding the birds in the park and Mally came jogging by. Naturally he stopped when he saw her. For days they'd been inseparable, but she woke up one morning to find him missing. The picture that last bit of information brought to my mind was more than I wanted to imagine.

"Maybe he just went back to work," I said, not having the slightest idea what I might be talking about.

"Mostly he's on call," she said. "He works personnel and maintenance for his mother's steam room business. He can pretty much work when he wants to, although he has to be there when they really need him. Besides, he wouldn't just take off. He would have told me where he was going and when he'd be back." Her fingers twisted again. "It's been three days, Jake. *Please* find him for me."

Let's face it, the word *please* coming from that beautiful mouth was all it took. I agreed to do whatever she wanted. I did, however, up the amount of the per diem I'd quoted her last time, a minor salve to my ego. She agreed.

"Did you go to the steam room looking for him?"

"Noooo....his mother doesn't know about us yet and maybe...." I let it go.

For the next half hour I listened to more of her Mally saga, asking questions and putting her answers in my pocket notebook, noting names, address, and possibilities. I also got a photograph so I'd know him if I found him. It seemed like the Patty Bird story all over again, only this time it was a human bird who had flown the coop. It was difficult to believe *any* man would go out of this woman's life.

Finally she illuminated me again with her smile and walked back out of my office. My heart felt heavy, and my stomach growled in frustration. Or was it hunger? I tried a hunger-fix with by opening a can of vegetable beef soup and set it directly on the hot plate. While it heated, I paced the room, too at-odds to hold still. I used the time to do some wishful thinking that Mally might just be involved with some new female conquest, while seemed unlikely, or the possibility that he'd been mugged.

When the soup had filled up the cracks in my hunger, I headed out the door for some interviews.

Mally's mother had an office in her steam room business called Drenched Ducks in the Wood Building on Twenty-Fourth. The receptionist wore one of those drab, formless dresses that left you with no knowledge of what was underneath. "Jake Whittaker, IRS," I said to Ms. Drab Dress, emphasizing the IRS part. That always gets immediate attention. I waited a couple of seconds to see if she'd ask for proof of who I was. When she foolishly didn't, I said, "I understand that Ms. Ducks owns this place."

She nodded.

"And I understand that she's about to file bankruptcy."

This time she violently shook her head. "No way. I keep the books, and Ducks is as solvent as a blue chip stock."

I ignored that. "I also understand," I said, "that she allows men and women wearing nothing but a towel to steam together." It wasn't an IRS concern, but Jake Whittaker just wondered.

"Boy, you sure don't know Mama Ducks. She's so straight-laced that evil rolls off her like water off a duck's back." She laughed at her own play on words.

"And the people who work for her?"

"Straight-laced or they're out the door." She finally thought about the questions I was asking and said, "What's this got to do with the IRS?"

"Just testing her integrity."

"Well, I can tell you, she's pure integrity. And if you heard any rumors about so-called massages taking place at Drenched Ducks, well, it's just not true. I think Harry at Harry's Hots, the steam room on Ponderosa, started that rumor because he's jealous."

"Jealous of what?"

"Of Drenched Ducks' success. We get all the female customers because they know they won't get hit on here. We also get the guys who only want to lose a few pounds and clean out their pores." Then she raised her eyebrows and said, "Harry gets the perverts who want the massages you-know-where."

I began to wonder how I'd ever missed the steam room scene, not sure if I was more suited to Ducks' or Harry's, but I looked Ms. Drab Dress in the face and chucked my tongue to show her I agreed about the massages.

"Ducks is a clean operation in more ways than one," she said. "The books are the same way. We pay our taxes and have nothing to hide." She looked down at a button lit up on the phone. "Mrs. Ducks is on the phone right now, but I'm sure she'll see you as soon as she's free." She handed me a small brochure. "Meanwhile, go on and check the place out for yourself. Why not try a steam while you're here? You'll have to pay, though. We do things above board here."

"If a steam bath tells me more about the business, then I think I'll do exactly that," I said. Why not?

I paid a fee and put a deposit down on a large red-striped towel. And so I left Ms. Drab Dress to go unclog my pores.

The men's locker room was sparse but clean, with two of the showers in use and a couple of other guys in stages of either dressing or undressing. There were lots of those little metal lockers where you could lock up your clothes, if you brought your own padlock. I stuffed my clothes inside locker number twenty-six because that was the age I was when I started working toward my P.I. license. I didn't have a padlock, but I doubted if anyone wanted my wrinkled khakis, patterned shirt, and scuffed shoes. My wallet, though, ended up between my skin and the towel I wrapped around me. Then I padded along damp floors in my bare feet as I headed for the men's steam room.

I closed the stream room door quickly behind me to keep in the steam, but someone must have just thrown water on the hot rocks. Steam was as thick as swamp fog. I groped my way to a bench, hoping like hell I didn't land a hand on someone's bare skin and get thrown out, or beaten up as a pervert. The air cleared about the same time I was settling my toweled butt onto the slats of a bench. It figures.

There were three other guys in the room, two of them flabby and happily sweaty, the other one was muscular with a determined, calm look. That also figures. I was getting the once-over before they resumed their conversation, so I concentrated on watching gravity pull water drops down the walls.

"First time, huh?" Flabby One said to me.

"How could you tell?"

"There's a look," he said, "and obviously you didn't know enough to bring your own towel." He pointed to the Ducks towel I was wrapped in. "You won't get your deposit back, you know."

I know I looked indignant. "I'm gonna return the towel," I said.

"Yeah, but then you get charged a washing fee exactly the same amount as the deposit."

"Oh," I murmured, looking down at the towel around my loins. I looked up at Flabby One and said, "Since you're all old pros here, what can you tell me about this place, as opposed to, say, Harry's Hots?"

Flabby Two jumped right in. "Forget Harry's. This place here may nickel and dime you to death, but at least the perverts and voyeurs are quickly weeded out."

"That receptionist out there didn't look like she'd be able to control a gaggle of senior citizens let alone a determined pervert."

That's when Muscle Guy chimed in. "Mally's the official bouncer. It's his mother's business. Mally has a cell phone and he can get here pretty damn fast. Mama calls and he comes.

"She your Mama, too?"

That brought a round of laughter from all three men. Flabby One even slapped his knee and sent a stream of water splashing my way. Flabby Two said, "Hell no, she ain't nobody's Mama except Mally's, but she tells everyone to call her that and, well, when Mama tells you to do something, you do it."

"She's mean?"

"No," Muscle Guy said, "but there's just something about Mama . . ."

". . . that makes you toe the line," Flabby Two finished up. That was the second time someone had said Mama liked people toeing the line.

"Mally, too?" I said.

"Oh yeah, Mally too."

"If I wanted to talk to Mally, where would I find him?"

Muscle Guy sat up straight, glanced over at the other two and grinned. "You might try making a pass at me. That oughta get Mally here in a hurry to kick your butt to kingdom come." This time the laughter was full of boyish delight of violence at my expense. I acknowledged Muscle Guy's joke with a smirk.

But it also gave me an idea. I waited through several minutes more of sweat dripping off my hair and into my eyes before I hefted myself off the bench and headed for the door. "The stream rolled out of the room with me, and I heard a chorus of "Close the door!" as I left.

I showered and dried off the best I could with a towel already damp with steam. There were only two other guys in the locker room, both sitting on a bench while they dressed. It was perfect for what I had planned.

I took my towel out to the receptionist. She was about to reach for it when I leaned in close. "In the men's locker room," I said, "there is a couple who . . ." I raised an eyebrow like I was talking about something I didn't dare say out loud.

"Two men?" she asked.

"No, a man and a woman."

"There's a woman in the men's room?" It wasn't really a question, it was a possibility that she wasn't about to accept.

"Yeah, and I couldn't tell if she's a willing participant or not."

"Damn!" she said and pushed a button under her desk.

A woman who had over ten years on me came out of a door behind the desk. She had one of those short hair-dos where every hair is the same length and all the curls are neighborly. Her dress—not pants, mind you—hit just below the knees. Prim and proper. Mama Ducks, I presumed. Ms. Drab Dress whispered to her, and they both glanced my way and whispered again. Then Mama took off like a bullet toward the men's locker room. *This should be interesting,* I said to myself as she hesitated in front of the door. She couldn't barge right in the men's locker, but she needed to know what might be going on in there.

She knocked.

A head poked out the door. She obviously asked her question. His face showed surprise before he looked back into the locker room, shook his head, and said something back at her. Then he opened the door wide for her to take a quick look. After a few more words, she came back to the desk. "Are you sure?" she asked me. "There's no female in there now."

"There was," I answered. "Behind that last row of lockers, back by the emergency exit door. She probably got in — and left — that way."

"If anyone opens that door, an alarm sounds."

"Well, where else could she have gone?"

"Maybe the alarm system has a malfunction," she said, mostly to herself. "I'll have Mally check it."

"Who's Mally? He your alarm contractor?"

"He's my son."

"You sure it wasn't Mally back there with a friend? He'd know how to override the alarm to get her in there in the first place."

The look I got was pure disgust. It was like a slap in the face.

"*How dare you!*" she sputtered. "My Mally is pure and innocent. He would never . . ." She faced me down like a mother lion and said, "And just who are you anyway?"

"IRS. There was some discrepancy in your last tax return, and I'm here to check it out."

She wasn't buying it. "I don't think so," she said. "And if you're IRS, let me see your ID."

When I just smiled sheepishly, she yelled, "I thought so. Get out of here, whoever you are. I don't ever want to see your face in here again. If Mally were here, I'd have him throw you out on the street."

"So where is Mally?"

She didn't bother with that one. She took a step closer to me, telling me to move on, or else. This Mama wasn't small, and she didn't look weak. I suddenly realized why people toed the line when Mama said toe.

My toes headed for the door.

★★★

A lot of P.I. work is at times boring and repetitive. Sitting in my car and watching the entrance to Drenched Ducks was one of those times. It gave me time to develop heartburn from the cold, limp salami sandwiches I like but my stomach doesn't. It also gave me time to think about what I might say to Mally if and when I found him. The wait could be a long one. He could be out of town on business or sacked out with someone other than Melissa, although my psyche couldn't imagine that. Either way, I wasn't having any success matching his picture to anyone who walked into Drenched Ducks.

When Ducks closed, I needed something to offset a boring day, and I took it as a good omen when I found a parking spot almost directly in front of Loretta and Cora Lee's place over the produce store. A twinge of guilt reminded me that Loretta had found the place herself after I'd promised to help locate one but never did.

Inside Cora Lee greeted me with hugs that made my day even if it was a little much. Then she grabbed my hand to show me her very own bedroom. Her books had finally found a home of their own. "Mama said we can afford to get pink paint for my walls now." She swept her hand around and said, "Everything in here will be pink, the walls, my sheets, and the curtains. Won't it be beautiful, Jake?"

I ignored that question. Pink and I don't see eye to eye. Then I realized there was only one bedroom in the apartment. "Where does your Mama sleep?" I asked.

"On the couch, just like you do," she said. "Isn't that great?" Only a kid could think it is great to sleep on a couch with the seams between the cushion making dents in your back.

She dragged me back to the boxy living room with only the couch and a table and two chairs. There was a kitchen the size of a breadbox, with the refrigerator under the small counter between the two-burner stove right next to a small sink.

Loretta was stirring a pot. She turned and flipped a hand at me. "Hi, Jake," she said. "I made stew. Want to stay and eat with us?"

She saw me look at the two chairs at the table. "Yeah, but...?" I said.

Cora Lee didn't let that question linger. "You and Mama can sit at the table," she said. "I like to sit on the couch, honest I do. Please say you'll stay."

"Okay, I'll stay."

"Yea!"

All I can say is that stew was either the best I've ever had, or it tasted doggone good because I was enjoying it almost like a family would. It was most satisfying to swirl some bread around my bowl afterwards to slop up every ounce of flavor.

After dinner I joined Cora Lee on the couch while Loretta cleaned up the dishes. Cora Lee grabbed a book and said, "Look, I got a new book. Want me to read it to you?"

No, I didn't. I was sure I would be hearing about some cat in a red-and-white striped hat who needed his back end paddled. She saw my head shaking. "Please, Jake. Please, please, *please*!"

The next think I knew, I was caught up in a story of an elf-like creature named Sogger who came in out of the rain and got everything wet. And I was almost sorry when Loretta said it was time for Cora Lee's bath before bed. Almost sorry it was time to leave.

There were three smiles in that small apartment as I was leaving. One of them was mine.

★★★

Melissa had said Mally was a morning jogger, so very early the next morning I headed for Dabbling Park where Mally had first seen Melissa. This time my stakeout was on one of the wooden benches that surrounded the jogging track, and this time my stomach applauded my breakfast choice of roast beef deli sandwiches. Two of them.

The second day of solitude was too much, though, so I started conversations with a couple of joggers who made the mistake of stopping near me to catch their breath.

One was a diminutive little pony-tailed female in black sweats and running shoes that had seen more miles than my broughams. "Can I ask you a couple questions?" I said. She shrugged and sat at the opposite end of the bench, ready to take off, I'd guess, if I hit on her in any way. "I'm looking for my friend Mally," I said. "Tall guy with tight muscles."

I pulled out his picture, and she nodded. "And he's got an even tighter family." I frowned like I didn't understand. "Yeah, I know Mally," she said, "and so do some of the other females running this track. He's a sweet guy but one to stay away from."

"Why's that?"

"Mally's got a mother, Mama she's called, who's a friggin' piranha. She eats his little playmates for breakfast the morning after, if you get what I mean. I swear she thinks he's a virgin, and nobody, but nobody, is good enough to deflower her Mally. I doubt if she'd even let him dabble with a wedding ring on his finger."

"So Mally talks a good story but doesn't dabble?"

"Hell yes, he dabbles! He picked me up right here in Dabbling Park." She burst out in nervous laughter. "He's not only a great dabbler, he's fun to talk to, too." Then her face got more serious, and she said, "But when Mama gets downwind of a new relationship, she sharpens her teeth and draws blood."

"Draws blood how?" My mind winced as I remembered the flawless skin surrounding Melissa.

"Depends on who's telling the tale. It could be an almost-mugging, a scary phone call, or, if you're lucky, maybe she keeps Mally out of sight until his latest passes on to easier liaisons."

"He puts up with all of that?"

"Boy Charming evidentially isn't into confrontation. Like everyone else, he toes the mark with Mama."

With that she learned forward, resting her arms on her legs while she thought. Then she turned to look directly into my face. "Hey, if Mally's a friend of yours, how come you don't know all this?"

I looked as sheepish as I felt. "Okay," I said, "so we're not that close, just friendly enough for him to borrow money he hasn't paid back. And now he's run aground somewhere besides at Drenched Ducks."

"It figures. He hasn't been here for over a week. You might try the track at Elder Park" Good grief, was everything around here named after ducks! She added, "Elder Park is another one of his breeding grounds. But I gotta tell ya, his M.O. is to wander off by himself once he's dabbled for a few days—unless Mama draws blood first."

With that she stood up and jumped in place for a few steps before heading out again on the track.

★★★

The jogging track at Elder Park was more of a path, without the quarter mile markers for the serious joggers at Dabbling. And the benches were concrete this time, cold and rough. I lowered myself onto one of them and hoped I hadn't already missed Mally.

The thought was no sooner out of my head when a tall guy in a gray sweat suit with a green hoodie came running around the bend. I won't tell you what I was thinking when I saw the size of his running shoes—or the size of the confident look he gave the good-looker running beside him. Bingo!

Poor Melissa.

Without knowing I was going to do it, I found myself standing up and yelling, "You Mally?"

They both stopped and jogged in place. "Yeah, so?" he said.

Okay, he was big, but I figured he was also used to following orders. "So sit," I said. "We need to talk."

He turned toward Good Looker. She looked back at him, looked at me, and took off down the path by herself.

He sat down on the bench. "Who're you? Mama send you to find me?"

Ah ha, so even Mama didn't know where he was this time. The expression on his face was hard and almost defiant. I got right to the heart of the matter. "The name Melissa mean anything to you?"

His face softened. "Oh yeah," he said. "You an ex-boyfriend?"

"Seems to me that's a description of you. You cut out on her."

"I'm going back just as soon as I figure out a way to explain to Mama that things have got to change."

I pointed down the path the way the female runner had gone. "Oh sure, it looks like you're pinning away for Melissa."

"I never saw her before today. She asked if she could run with me, that's all."

I let that go. "But you think Mama's gonna understand this time, huh, because it's Melissa? I don't buy it. And I don't buy it that you give two hoots about Melissa other than in the bedroom. You left her *three days ago*, cowboy. What's a broken heart to you?"

He was quiet for a moment. Finally he looked directly at me and said, "I needed time to think. Melissa's different."

I certainly wasn't going to argue with that.

"I didn't expect it," he said, "but we've fallen in love. I could never hurt her."

"Too late," I said. I was thoroughly disgusted with him. I saw him as somebody who wasn't into commitment, and Mama would never allow it anyway. But he was also the Somebody Melissa Loved. Damn!

Then I did something I seldom do. I broke a P.I. rule and told Mally who I really am and why I was there. I laid out how Melissa didn't deserve a low-life like him and that my report to her was going to contain my opinion as well as the damning facts. He listened with his head down. I ended with a question full of contempt. "And just when did you plan on going back to her?"

He answered by pulling a small box from the pocket of his sweat pants. The hinged top swung up to reveal a knockout diamond ring. "Today," he said. "I have to get up the nerve to show this to Mama first, before I give it to Melissa."

"Oh sure! I'll believe that when I see it."

His lips pursed. "Okay," he said, "come with me to talk to Mama." Surprise, must have registered on my face. "I mean it," he said. "You come with me to straighten this out with Mama first, and I'll make your report to Melissa myself, including all the unflattering facts."

It only took me a second to make a decision.

★★★

"Mally!" Ms. Drab Dress shouted, as she reached for the button under her desk.

Mama came out of the office and lit up like a flare. "Darling, you're back," she said. There was only a fleeting frown when she saw me before she turned back to her son.

"Mama, we gotta talk."

She flipped her head toward me and said, "All right. Throw this bum out first and we'll go into my office."

Mally folded his arms across his chest. "He stays. This is Jake Whittaker, and he's going to be a witness to what I have to say." She seemed to back down a little and led Mally into her office, ignoring me as I followed behind. She and I sat down, but Mally paced.

"Mama," he said, "things are gonna change."

She waited silently as he pulled the ring box out of his pocket, flipped it open, and held it in front of her face.

All the color drained out of her. "Whaaat . . .?" she sputtered.

This time he backed down a little. "It's only a friendship ring, Mama. Her name's Melissa. Maybe later, down the road, it'll be an engagement ring."

"Never!" she spat out. "No way!"

She startled the bee-jeebers out of both of us. I could see now how Mama drew the line for everyone to toe. For a moment Mally looked like he was about to knuckle under again, but then he handed her a picture. "This is Melissa, Mama. She's as beautiful inside as she is outside."

Mama looked at the picture, but the expression on her face didn't change.

"Ms. Ducks," I said, "can I have a word here?" She shot a look at me like a bug had just spoken, but she let me continue. "Look," I began, "wouldn't you like to have someone to be like a daughter you could teach how to cook?" It was the first thing that came to mind.

"I don't cook."

Shit!

"Okay," I said, trying to think fast. "Think about having a daughter-in-law, down the road somewhere, who will give you grandchildren. They'll be beauties if they take after Mally and Melissa."

The look on her face softened.

Mally jumped in. "Look, Mama," he said, "our name is Ducks. You named me Mallard and you call the business Drenched Ducks. We both choose to live near Dabbling and Elder Parks because they're duck names. You love ducks, Mama, and Melissa is not only one sweet duck but her middle name is a family name of Drake!"

Damn if she didn't look like she was melting. She turned from steel to clay right before my eyes. "Drake?" she muttered.

Mally nodded and then looked to me for what to say next.

"Call Melissa," I said. "Let your Mama meet the mother of her future grandchildren." Mama said nothing as Mally took out a cell phone and turned his back on both of us.

While they waited for Melissa to show up, Mally and his Mama sat knee-to-knee in two chairs, laying out future plans. Me? I just waited to get one last look at Melissa before I took off to do lonely P.I. stuff.

As I waited, I planned my report to Melissa with the corrupted words of an old ditty my Mama sang to me:

> Be kind to your web-footed friends,
> For a Ducks maybe somebody's mother,
> You two in your love will be fine,
> But with Mama you'll *both* toe the line.

> You may think that this is the end.
> Well, it is!

CHAPTER 13
ALMOST LIKE FAMILY

"Hey, Jake, you wanna go to a pancake breakfast?" Cora Lee poked her head through the office door with an elfish grin on her face. This wasn't someone I wanted to see. She might be bringing me another case that I knew I didn't want to consider, even if my time was open and my wallet empty. Cora Lee is cute but cunning, and I wasn't into connecting with that. No one with any sense likes kids. But, what the hell, kids don't come any entertaining than Cora Lee.

"Where'd you come from?" I asked. "Where's your Mama?"

"Mama's downstairs, waiting for us. Come on, Mr. Cramer said I could bring a friend. He's going to pick us up here in five minutes."

"Hold on a second, Squirt. What are you talking about? Slow down and tell me who Mr. Cramer is."

She gave a sigh of disgust and plunked herself down in the client chair in front of my desk. "He's one of the accountants Mama works for." Both ends of her mouth turned way up as she leaned forward and whispered, "I think he likes Mama a whole lot."

Well, well, well. Whoever Mr. Cramer was, he certainly had good taste. "So what's with this pancake breakfast stuff?"

That got another sigh, like she knew I wouldn't understand even if she told me.

"You know, pancakes, all you can eat, with butter and syrup. Maybe sausages. Some animal is making them."

She was right, I didn't understand.

"Some animal?"

"Yeah, an elk."

"Oh, you mean the Elks Club."

"Yeah, them."

She jumped up, came around behind the desk, and grabbed my hand. "Come on, Jake. It's pancakes."

I went. How could I not?

★★★

"Jake," Loretta said, "this is Carl Cramer. Carl, Jake Whitter." We shook hands.

"Loretta tells me you do private investigations," Mr. Cramer said to me in the car. Not one to miss an opportunity, I fished a business card out of my pocket and handed it up to the front seat for him. He waved it in the air as he said, "Mind if I call you later?"

"Sure, or I can come to your place," I said, not sure I wanted an accountant to see how I lived in my office and slept on the couch there. We left it at that.

At the Elks Club I held back, waiting to see what Cramer would do. It was also my chance to get a good look at him. He was trim and younger than I am, but then most days I feel older than I really am. He was looking like what he probably was, an accountant on a day off.

His hair had to have been "styled," not hacked off like mine. His sports coat had to be silk, and his shoes had tassels on them. Somehow, though, there was only confidence, not swagger, in his walk. He walked up to the cashier, handed him a bill, and said, "Four please." Fancy that. Cramer was generous as well as stylish. We followed him as he ushered us to a table with four empty chairs.

Cora Lee skipped along, followed by me, a guy who felt like the first day of school where you don't know anyone and aren't sure you want to. Once seated, though, both Cora Lee and I were in our element: food. We even each accepted a second plate of pancakes, with butter and syrup generously slavered over the whole plate. Her appetite was almost as good as mine. I managed six sausages; she only managed four.

Cramer and Loretta talked together across the table from us. I could see that Loretta had a smitten look on her face. I just hoped Cramer wasn't leading her down some garden path.

Cora Lee ran a talking marathon on me until my ears turned red, and I only half listened. She talked about a new park near their new apartment, she talked about some kid named Harry who was a potter, and she talked about some TV show where people fought to outdo each other. "This one mean guy pushed this woman out of his way," she said. "That wasn't nice, was it, Jake?"

"You have a TV now?" I asked.

"Yeah. Mr. Cramer got it for us. He said no one should be without a TV."

"He paying for the cable, too?"

"No, Mama said she'd pay if I could wait a little longer to get paint for my bedroom."

Hmm, the relationship between Loretta and Cramer must have future possibilities. I'd never given a girl more than a dinner and movie.

It was then I learned that the boredom from being stuck in an office/home can sometimes be superior to listening to endless prattle from a kid who was cuter than a button but never learned to button up.

★★★

A knock on my door brought me out of my nap. A waited a second for my voice to not show I'd been sleeping before I said, "It's open."

It was Cramer. He waved the business card I'd given him.

I took a quick looking around, hoping my place wasn't a complete mess. Not knowing what to say, I pointed to the client chair across from my desk. "Good to see you again," I began. "Something I can do for you?"

"I need help."

"What kind of help? And why me? I imagine you could get one of the big agencies downtown."

"I have to be discreet. Big firms might have big mouths, and I can't chance it."

I waved again at the client chair and said, "My mouth is so small I can hardly brush my teeth, let alone spit out anything about a client. So, tell me, what can I help you with?"

"My firm is Cramer and Rhodes, CPAs. Rhodes and I have been in business for eleven years as equal partners, and until recently we were doing well." He hesitated for a moment and then added, "Well, we're still doing well, but I sense we're not bringing in new clients like we used to." When I just nodded like I understood, he continued, "Now I see Rhodes here and there with people who look like clients but I've never seen them in our office. I wonder if he's shorting me on money by taking on clients apart from the firm. Our bottom line doesn't seem to match with our cliental."

"You're an accounting firm. Don't you do your own books?"

"Partly we do, but we have an off-site bookkeeper to keep us from what I think is happening lately. Our overhead is fairly low. Besides office rent, we just have one secretary between us and Loretta who's our receptionist."

I thought about it for a moment. "The people you see Rhodes with, are they male or female?"

"Both, but what difference does that make?"
"Females could be girlfriends?"
He looked taken aback. "But he's married!"
I just looked at him like *Soooo*....

He shrugged, then added, "I've seen him with several different women in a restaurant, talking like accountant and client, not lovey-dovey."

"And the men?"

"Same thing."

"All right, but what exactly do you want me to do? How do you expect me to find out if he has clients on the side that aren't going through your books?"

He started to speak, but I held up my hand and said, "Hold it, what if I became a possible 'side' client with Rhodes? "

He thought about that and said, "That might do it."

"Tell me where I might be able to meet him and broach the subject. If he takes me on, we'll see if he turns me in as a client."

His grin told me that I had a viable scenario.

For the next twenty minutes Cramer gave me three pages of info in my pocket notebook. I got a picture of Harold Rhodes and a list of places he frequented. I began to picture myself as an actor making inroads into the secret life of Harold Rhodes. Right up my alley, even if I wasn't sure I could get out of my alley environment and look like I'm an accounting culture client.

Cramer had been generous with a TV for Loretta and Cora Lee, so I figured I could get away with doubling my per diem, plus expenses. He went for it. He pushed a wad of bills across the desk. It was either personal funds or he didn't want my fee going through his company's books. It worked for me.

Cramer left after giving me a description of Rhodes.

I shuffled through the business cards I had pilfered from here and there. I needed to be someone I'm not. Either the businesses—or the names—didn't seem right, so I sifted through some cards in my own name that Freddie, the computer geek kid, had made for me. They were a multitude of different businesses. It was a sunshiny day, so I selected one for a flower shop and one for a health food store. That last one was Freddie's sense of humor.

★★★

Of course I didn't get to work right away. Some things are more important, and Frank's bar is one. As I perched on my usual bar stool, I slid several bills across the bar to Frank. "I figure this should just about wipe out my tab," I said. Frank, being his usual mute self, just smiled, picked up the bills, and plunked down a beer in front of me. Life doesn't get any better than being current on my bar bill and having a job that promises good money with, hopefully, little effort. And I didn't want to forget to be thankful for the good, foamy taste of cold beer.

Dessert first, then the main course.

★★★

Cramer had told me that Rhodes was an art lover and would be going to an exhibit that night, so I dolled myself up as much as possible and prepared to look like a possible art buyer. Doggone if I didn't find myself back that evening at the art gallery where Dahlia Duncan had her exhibit of ocean scene paintings. She wasn't there, thank goodness, and neither was Brooks with his self-help books. This exhibit was a lot classier than last time. This time they were featuring an artist who painted more than the ocean.

It was late afternoon, and several plates of snacks were already on the table, along with several open bottles of wine. This time the food had more character than last time, and the wine had corks rather than screw tops. I love it when I can mix work with my appetite. I hardly noticed the paintings on the walls once I had my mouth full of pinwheel sandwiches and cheese something-a-others.

People were still filtering in when I started walking around with one hand holding a plate of one-of-each and the other hand wrapped around a glass of whatever red wine was already open.

I had to look like an art lover while I waited for Rhodes to show up. I pretended to be interested in painting after painting—boringly, endlessly. Two plates of food and one wine refill later, a guy who fit Rhodes description finally showed up. He was a carbon copy of Cramer. His silk suit was definitely not off-the-rack and he had a determined look that would make a mugger think twice about approaching him.

I gave him minutes to schmooze a little and start his progression around the paintings. By this time I'd put my plate and wine glass on a table with other dirty dishes.

When Rhodes stopped in front of a painting of an abandoned cabin in a field of poppies, I figured I had an "in" with my flower shop business card.

I stepped beside him and ventured, "Ever see a field of poppies like that?"

"Yeah, but they only bloom one short period a year."

"I only like flowers that people need to pay for," I ventured.

"How's that?"

"I own a flower shop a couple towns over. It does pretty well, but there's too much paperwork. I hate paperwork!"

He reached in his pocket for a small leather folder of business cards and handed a card to me. I glanced at it and read, "Harold Rhodes, CPA" with an address that hadn't been on Cramer's card with both their names. "You work alone?" I asked. He nodded.

Bingo! I probably had him on that business card alone, but I wanted more for Cramer. Besides, half a day's work wasn't going to pay my rent.

"Maybe I *could* use a bookkeeper," I said.

"I'm not a bookkeeper; I'm a CPA," he said.

"So you don't do bookkeeping?"

He turned a dazzling smile on me and said, "For a guy who likes flowers like you do, I'll be a bookkeeper. You got a card?"

I smiled back at him, reached into my pocket, and gave him a card. He looked at it and said, "What's this? I thought you said you owned a flower shop? You're a private investigator?"

Damn! Without thinking, I'd handed him my regular business card. I'd blown my cover. Damn! Damn! Damn!

I tried to cover it by saying, "That, too." His face showed he didn't understand any better than I did. "You see . . ., " I began, "I *am* an investigator, but I also own the flower shop. That's why I need your help. I'm so busy investigating that I don't have time for flower shop bookkeeping, and none of my employees are qualified." Oh, good one, Whittaker. I almost convinced myself.

Rhodes looked a little rattled, but I think he bought it. Then his eyes showed that his brain was buzzing. He looked directly at me and said, "How about a deal? I want to get some dirt on someone, and you could help me with that. In turn, I'll give you a real rate on your bookkeeping."

"What kind of dirt?"

"Look, this is definitely info under the table, but I need dirt on a guy. You know, like *personal* tax invasion or taking money from a client's escrow account. I need what might be considered immoral—or at least unethical." He leaned n close and said, "You understand. I need to have a hold over him, if you know what I mean."

I gave a knowing smile and asked again, "Who's going to know what I turn up besides you?"

"Just me. Any info you get for me would be strictly between you and me."

My lips pursed as in thought and I said, "Sounds like a win-win deal." I nodded my head like I was in line with his request. Then I got to the nitty-gritty.

"What's this guy's name?" I asked.

"Carl Cramer."

My knees buckled, and I almost fell. My mind raced for some kind of order. I may not have a whole lot of scruples, but having opposing clients is not in my portfolio. I needed time to think. "This really isn't the place," I said. "How about we meet tomorrow morning for coffee and get this thing started?" When he nodded, I named the time and The Hot Cup coffee shop where Loretta had worked before she got the receptionist gig. I think better in familiar surroundings. Right then my mind wasn't cooperating at all.

★★★

I had to think, so it was back to Frank's bar. It wasn't too busy when I got there, with a little angel on one shoulder shouting across to the little devil on my other shoulder, I was stone quiet as I motioned to Frank for a cold one. I gulped down half of it before the angel and devil called it a truce. Still, my stomach wasn't cooperating, so I tried to drown that jumpy feeling with salted nuts Frank put by my beer. Frank knows me well.

Could I take on two clients who were out to get each other? Was that kosher? Would it end in a Mexican standoff? Would I be in the middle when the bullets started flying? None of my questions got answered, even after two more beers.

★★★

I got to The Hot Cup well before the time I was to meet Rhodes. Donna was there behind the counter. As I headed for a booth, I waved her over. She came with a little person beside her. I hadn't noticed Cora Lee. This complicated things. Donna I could count on to stay out of my meeting except as a waitress, but Cora Lee couldn't be counted on to not blurt out whatever was on her mind.

Cora Lee slid opposite me in the booth. "Jake!" she yelled. "Where have you been? Mama and I miss you."

"Yeah, yeah," I said. "But this isn't a social visit. I'm meeting someone, and you have to make yourself scarce."

She looked about to cry. "I never get in your way, Jake." She looked ready to cry. "I don't need you," she said. "I have Mama and Donna and Mr. Cramer." I could see the hurt on her face.

"No, no, you don't understand," I said. "You never get in the way." It was half lie and half truth, with neither side winning. "This is a job, you see. And I need to talk to the man without anyone interrupting us."

"Oh, okay," she said. Then she drew a finger across her chest two times and said, "Cross my heart."

"And why the . . . aren't you in school, young lady?"

I got a disgusted look. "It's Saturday, Jake." My head just bobbed back in forth like I should have known that.

Donna had stood there listening to us. She said, "Cross my heart, too." Then she motioned Cora Lee out of the booth and back to the counter. Donna I could trust, but Cora Lee, I knew, wouldn't take her eyes off me and off Rhodes when he arrived. I cursed myself for choosing this place to meet him. How stupid could I get?

Donna came over and slid a cup of coffee in front of me without either of us saying a word.

Rhodes walked in, looking out of place. This isn't a fancy restaurant or even a swanky coffee shop in an important hotel. He glanced around until he saw me in a booth and hurried over. His hand reached out as he slid into the bench seat. I shook it and said, "Tell me about this Cramer guy. Why's he on your hate list — and what are you going to do with whatever I dig up?"

"Cramer's stuck in a rut. He was detrimental to a business dealing I once had with him, with his straight-laced morals that no one would expect of anyone. All I want is a little payback. Legit, of course."

"Where am I to look? Online? With a business he has now? Friends, wife, colleagues? Who's going to talk to me about him?"

He reached in his coat pocket and handed me a folded paper. I unfolded it and saw names with addresses and phone numbers, along with their relationship to Cramer.

He said, "I don't want you to go to Cramer's business, that's why it isn't on the list. Cramer doesn't have a wife now, but I listed people who know or knew him well and might not really like the guy. Talk to them. See if something will erase Cramer's boy scout image."

"The flower shop does pretty good retail," I said, "but I keep that separate from my investigative work. I'm sure I can carry out your directive, but I'll need a retainer—and expenses, of course."

He didn't bat an eye. He pulled out a checkbook and started writing. Tearing the check out, he handed it to me and said, "How's that for a start?"

Good golly, I could catch up on all my debts and maybe even buy a new suit! "It'll do," I said. I think I impressed even myself with my blasé manner.

"Deal!" I said. "I'm going to start as soon as I finish my coffee. I'll be in touch."

We shook hands again, and he walked out. I watched through the window as he climbed into a Lexus and drove off.

Cora Lee came skipping over with a plate of two donuts and said, "Did I do okay, Jake, did I?"

"You did just fine, Sweetheart." I got that evil eye from her and said, "I know, I know, you're not my sweetheart. Can I just call you Silly One?"

She thought about it and said, "Sure. Silly is good."

We both grabbed a donut and got our mouths full.

★★★

The name on Rhodes list that I figured had the most potential was Cramer's ex-wife. Well, well, Cramer had an ex-wife, huh? Not that it would make any difference to Loretta, and Cora Lee had already glommed on to him.

The small craftsman house on a quiet street had a manicured yard and a small front porch with a rocking chair and a side table. The rocking chair held a woman in jeans and T-shirt, reading a book. Cramer's ex-wife, I hoped.

As I walked up the walk to the porch, I said, "Are you Mrs. Cramer?"

"I was, but I'm not any more. Who's asking?"

"Jake Whittaker." I had no idea how to continue from there. I'm not one for thinking ahead, I guess. Her face just showed more wonder, so I said, "I'm here to investigate regarding a new insurance policy for Mr. Cramer. Do you mind if I sit here on the step and ask you a couple of questions?"

She laid the open book face down on the table and waved a hand toward the steps. I climbed to porch level and plunked myself down.

"What can you tell me about Mr. Cramer?" I asked.

"A little of everything. What does insurance have to do about anything?"

"Well, Ma'am, does he have any long-term health problems?"

"Hell no, he's a health nut. But he does like sweets." My mind popped up with a vision of Cora Lee and Cramer over a plate of donuts. I felt a little left out, but I quickly smothered the thought and said, "What about his work? Is he — was he — in a dangerous job?"

"The only thing dangerous about being in the financial business is hooking up with a immoral partner." She was quiet for a moment and added, "Sometimes we all make lousy choices, and mine was divorcing Carl."

I put it right on the line and blurted out, "Why did you?"

"Well, it's none of your business, and it has nothing to do with insurance, I assure you. Let's just put it that I got bored and didn't know how to get un-bored." She waved at her book, and the house, and the general neighborhood and added, "And here I am, still bored!"

"Is there anything you can tell me that might put Mr. Cramer in a bad light? Maybe an addiction? A secret life? An indiscretion? A small crime?

She laughed. "Hardly. At least those things wouldn't have been boring!"

"I think I get the picture, Ma'am. Carl Cramer isn't likely to be killed by something made to look like an accident. Is his business a success?"

"It was. He and his partner Rhodes had a good thing going. But the grape vine tells me that the business is floundering now. You should talk to Mr. Rhodes. He can probably tell you things I can't. But I suspect that Rhodes is . . . well, I think I'll keep my mouth shut."

"Mr. Rhodes might have something against your ex-husband?"

"It might be the other way around," she said. Then she picked up her book and let me know that I was being excused.

I thanked her for the help and headed back to my car, thinking no one — that's *no one* — is as squeaky clean as the ex-wife was spouting about Carl Cramer. But I hoped it was mostly true for Loretta's and Cora Lee's sake.

★★★

I should be given credit here. The next place I headed was just two blocks from Frank's bar, and I didn't even think of stopping in there. Chalk up one for me!

The weekly newspaper was called The Record. Unimaginative name but just what I was looking for. It was a wide store front in a busy strip mall. The publisher had his name on the window. I could see a counter for the public up front. A bell rang as I opened the door and walked up to a twenty-something closest to me. She was wearing a shirt that said "I DONT THIINK SO" and had a hairdo that wasn't thinking at all.

"Excuse me," I said. No one paid any attention. "Excuse me," I said in a louder voice. Twenty-something slapped her pencil down on her desk, telling me I was a nuisance.

She walked up to the counter, tried to smile, and said, "Yeah, what can I do for you?" It looked like I was about to have to pull some teeth to get anything out of her.

"I need to see your files on some articles."

"It ain't that easy, Mister. In the first place, we don't probably have files like you're thinking of, and in the second place, why should I get them for you?"

Ack! I should have stayed in bed this morning! "Why?" I said, as I dug in a back pocket to get a twenty to lay on the counter. "Because you look like a friendly soul who would like to help a citizen."

Her hand slid over the bill as she said, "What file do you have in mind?"

"Anything about a financial firm called Cramer and Rhodes."

She gave an annoying sigh and said, "Sit down. I'll have to go looking."

I sat and picked up a copy of The Record's last issue. News of the day in the neighborhood and a little beyond. Ads for businesses. Weekly columns that *somebody* might want to read. And there on the fifth page were the police proceedings for the previous week and court filings. Was there something juicy that had previously happened with Cramer and Rhodes that would help me out?

Just in time, Twenty-something came back to the counter and motioned for me to join her. She had a file in her hand.

"You'll have to come in here to read this," she said. "Not a page of it is to disappear." She opened a little gate and let me in behind the counter and over to an empty desk. "Don't mess up the order," she said, "and don't try to pocket anything. I'm watching." Then she left me with the file.

The file held dated articles from the newspaper on a suit against Cramer and Rhodes over a year ago. The law suit was filed against them for withholding a client's court-ordered settlement. The suit was dropped after the firm held a press conference where Cramer issued an apology on an oversight. Rhodes was nowhere to be seen at the conference. Another article listed a police report where Rhodes was accused of embezzling money from his son's Little League fundraiser. That one also showed Rhodes with a sheepish grin and a "look, I found the money," excuse. There was a follow-up article on a new holder of the Little League monies. The firm itself was in an article where they gave $1,000 to the Make a Wish organization. Okay, this was just after the dropped law suit, but I could understand that.

Enough was enough. I closed the folder and took it over to Twenty-Something. "It's all there," I said and walked out of the building.

★★★

I form my own opinions. At this point I was liking Cramer though holding back on complete trust. Rhodes? I diidn't like the guy. Smart but obviously out for himself only. I was wondering who I was going to give a report to when I finished. Or both of them? Good or bad? I didn't know. Geez.

So I did what I usually do when I need to think. I turned my mind off and took a nap, hoping the Sleep Fairy will have figured out what I need to do next.

★★★

The Cramer and Rhodes outside bookkeeper was next. The office was above a donut shop, and my shaky will power sent me right up the stairs without even looking in the donut window. Yea for me! Besides, donuts aren't the same without sharing them with Cora Lee.

The bookkeeper's office was one room with a multitude of file cabinets in metal gray. The one desk was full but had an organized look. One side had manila folders, with a pencil cup and electric pencil sharpener. The other side held a computer. A printer was on a side table.

Mary Jones was as generic as her name. She was as rounded as the usual female, wore pants and a shirt that could have come from any thrift shop, and her shoes were off her feet beneath her desk. A no-nonsense, trust-worthy type. She looked up as I came in. She held out a hand and said, "Hi, I'm Mary Jones, bookkeeper extraordinaire." Her smile was half grin. I liked her right with the get-go.

I handed her my P.I. card. There wasn't going to be any fooling with her. She looked at it, looked at me, and looked at the card again. "Your firm needs a bookkeeper?" she said.

"May I sit down?" I asked. She waved at the chair in front of the desk. I sat. Then I sighed and said, "I have a dilemma." Not knowing what to do, I opened up the whole story to her, leaving nothing out. I ended up with, "So, you see, I have two clients who have each hired me separately to get dirt on the other one. It doesn't say much for me, but there you have it."

"You know," she said, "that I can't tell you anything about Cramer and Rhodes or even what I think about them individually."

"Yeah, I know."

"But I can make a suggestion. It sounds like they each want to get out of their partnership agreement and want reasons to dissolve it that are listed in the agreement itself. Why don' you get the two of them together . . . "

"I can't let them know I'm two-timing each of them!"

"Get them together—or separately—and suggest that each one talk to the other one about agreeing to close out the partnership and split the assets, profits, and the obligations. A lawyer could help with that if they both agree to it."

Damn! Why hadn't I thought of that? Instead of being an investigator, I should have changed hats and become a problem solver. They aren't necessarily the same thing.

★★★

I didn't need to write a report to either Cramer or Rhodes. I didn't even need to list any expenses. I felt I'd been paid enough by each of them initially. Two phone calls and two short, separate meetings later, and they both agreed to see the *same* lawyer to dissolve the partnership. Son of a gun! Who'd of thunk it!

I was feeling like a proper business man when I headed over to The Hot Cup to see if Cora Lee might be there. I could afford to treat her to all the donuts she wanted—as long as she left a couple for me.

CHAPTER 14
WEDDING BELLS

My mail is delivered to a keyed box in the lobby of my office/residence. I don't get much mail. I hardly open the box unless I'm expecting a check. My last P.I. gig of several weeks ago for Cramer and Rhodes had left me ignoring my mail. But, what the hell, you never know how Uncle Sam might grace me with something besides advertisements and flyers.

I had a grocery store ad that told me I could get two kiwis for seventy-five cents. I don't even know what a kiwi is, except for the picture of a green something. Looks like fruit, but I don't eat fruit if I can help it. I tossed all the junk in the barrel there in the lobby.

I was left with two odd-sized envelopes, one white, one cream. No return addresses, the usual for sellers that want you to open them to see what might be inside. Okay, it worked. I opened the first one:

Miss Loretta Sinclair
And
Mr. Carl Cramer
Request Your Attendance
At Their Wedding
1:00 pm on November 22
At
The Ballroom of Hotel Paradise
(please bring this invitation)
RSVP At 555-2303

Wow, Loretta finally got a real break. I could imagine how happy Cora Lee would be. She seemed to love Cramer. He had gotten out of his partnership with Rhodes and started his own accounting firm. The dissolving agreement let clients decide who they wanted to stay with, and Cramer came out pretty good. He could take care of Loretta and Cora Lee. Maybe he even had enough mullah to buy out a donut shop for Cora Lee. I could even be an invited guest.

Hell yes, I'd go to their wedding. I'd even have my only suit dry cleaned.

Then I opened the second envelope. Good grief it was another wedding invitation.

Mrs. Geraldine Duck
Requests Your Attendance
At the Wedding of
Miss Melissa Allgood
and
Mr. Mallard Duck
3:00 pm on November 22
At
The Chapel at Dabbling Park
RSVP At 555-2869

My knees started shaking! No, no, no! That vision called Melissa was going out of my life? Forever? Mally caught the brass ring and had thrown it around Melissa. I am a bachelor and seemed doomed to remain one. Life isn't fair.

I looked at both invitations again. Both were on the same day, almost at the same time, just ten days away. What in the hell was I supposed to do? Split my personality and go to both at the same time? There was no way I could miss seeing Melissa one last time. Maybe seeing her with another man *permanently* would stop my nightly visions, but I doubted it. But if I missed Loretta's wedding, Cora Lee *would not* understand my not being there. I would be dead meat in her eyes.

I didn't want to think about it. I needed some sand to bury my head in. I needed to throw myself on the floor and have a tantrum. *I needed a beer!*

Fifteen minutes later I was sitting on a stool in front of a beer. "I don't know what to do," I said to Frank after telling him about the two wedding invitations. "I want to go to one happy wedding but can't also go to the unhappy—for me—wedding. What should I do?"

Frank just pursed his lips and didn't answer. I didn't expect him to, but he could have least have said, "Bummer!" He didn't.

"Gimme a hard-boiled egg," I said. "No, make it two. And put a ham sandwich in that thingy you grill on. I need food." Frank moved away to get my order.

"What's the problem?" a voice said? A female popped down into the stool beside me. "I heard you talking about a marriage. Yours?"

"No, two women friends."

"They're marrying each other?"

"No, two different guys."

"That's bad?"

"Well, one is a dream I missed out on, and the other is starting a life I probably never will get to start."

"Bummer!" she said. Ah, at last, someone who can fill in for Frank.

When I didn't offer any more, she just kinda shrugged and then moved back to her stool and left me to stuff myself with eggs and ham.

★★★

I made the call to Cramer's office to give my RSVP that I would attend the wedding. As my name was spoken back to me, the phone was grabbed, and I heard Cora Lee belt out, "Jake!" A warm chuckle came out of me. "Yeah, Kiddo, it's me, telling you that I wouldn't miss the wedding."

"Of course you wouldn't," she said. "And you're gonna love it. Mama has a new white dress she's going to wear. It goes all the way to the floor! Donna is going to stand by Mama with a lavender dress." She started talking faster and faster. "And, Jake, I'm gonna be up by Donna, and my dress will be lavender, too! And the room is big and will be beautiful with flowers and a 'zebo' thing where some guy will make them husband and wife. Isn't that wonderful?" "And, oh Jake, the food afterwards you will love. Meat, shrimp, little cream cheese sandwiches, and some salads. Of course you won't care about the salads, but . . ."

"Hold on, Chatty One! I get the idea. But please don't tell me that there won't be anything sweet."

"Silly, there will be a wedding cake three cakes high. All white with frosting flowers on it!"

"What, no donuts?"

"Maybe at breakfast the next day, because Donna said I can stay at her place for the week Mamma and Carl are in Las Vegas for a honeymoon. When Donna goes to work, I can sit and color at The Hot Cup. You will come see me at Donna's work, won't you?"

"I never could say no to a donut, you know that."

"Okay, Jake. They want their phone back now, so I gotta go. Bye."

"Bye," I said, but she was already gone. It's a good thing I don't really like kids, because I would miss Cora Lee right now if I did.

★★★

The invitation to Melissa's wedding sat on my desk. I knew I really shouldn't go. I wanted to go. Of course I wouldn't go. I wanted to go. I'd tell them I couldn't make it. I wanted to go.

I wanted to go. I didn't make the call; I left my options open.

The next day I was in my office looking in the file cabinet when Cora Lee came barging in. I pretended to ignore her, so she just ignored me, too. She took the book she had and sat down at my desk. She picked up the wedding invitation and said, "What's this?"

"Oh, are you here? Well, it's an invitation to a wedding the same day as your Mama's wedding."

"Is this about that lady who was missing her partridge bird?

"Yeah, it's her."

"You really like her, huh, Jake?'

I just shrugged.

"Would you go to her wedding if you weren't going to my Mama's wedding?"

I just shrugged again, and we left it at that.

★★★

For the next week I followed a man around, waiting to get a picture of him with someone who wasn't his wife. It was common P.I. work, and easy enough to do if you don't mind stagnant waiting and boredom. I mind 'em, but it's easy money. On Tuesday I followed his car and watched it turn into a sleazy outlying motel. Bingo! I parked at the convenience store next door, grabbed my mini camera, and walked over to the motel, trying to look like I was already registered. My prey had parked and was sitting in his car. What, no pre-registration? Oh, there, he got out and walked up to the registration office. I walked around like I was just doing a little walking exercise, keeping my camera in my pocket. Ten minutes later he came out with a key in his hand and climbed back into his car.

My exhausted legs were just about worn out when another car pulled in off the street and parked next to my guy. Bingo again! A slim woman in a short skirt and lacquered hair got out at the same time as my guy. I resurrected my camera just in time to snap a mushy kiss, hoping his face was visible. I made sure I got proof by snapping another picture as he opened the motel room, turned to face her with a smile (snap!), and they both entered the room, shut the door, and left me to hobble back to my car. I reminded myself to never exercise again.

I dropped memory thingy from my camera off at Kinkos and went home to pat myself on the back. My client would hate me for what I showed her later, but she would pay me. The wives always do.

★★★

As the two weddings day got closer, I still hadn't called Mrs. Duck to tell her I would or wouldn't be attending the wedding. How could I? But I wanted to. I let the problem fester. I picked up my suit and my only white shirt at the cleaners. I drank beer. I tried to talk to Frank, but he only filled my glass before going to the other end of the bar to talk to Kitty, his woman friend. That's *talk* to Kitty. He wasn't giving her any one-word conversation like he did with everyone else; he was *talking* to her in complete sentences! What was the world coming to?

I ordered a grilled sandwich. When it arrived on a paper plate, I smiled and wagged my head over Kitty's way. All I got from Frank was some sort of secret smile before he left me alone again. My thoughts turned to Loretta, Cora Lee, Melissa, and even Jolene from high school. I felt like some ship had sailed without me. Then Gramma showed up in my mind. *I love you, Jake,* was all she had to say, and I didn't mind the ship disappearing.

I had another beer.

★★★

I pushed the knot of my tie up to my collar, wishing I had a full-length mirror to get the total effect of my spiffy, clean gray suit. The men's room down the hall only had a mirror over the sink. I put a comb in one pants pocket and two tissues and some money in the other pocket. I slid my business cards into my inside suit jacket. Then I stood as though my file cabinet was a full-length mirror and said, *"Eat your heart out, Mally."* That's when I realized I was planning to get to Melissa's wedding somehow.

But Loretta's wedding came *now.*

Hell's bells, there was valet parking at Hotel Paradise. I was to show them my invitation, but, of course, I forget to bring it. "Ahh, come on," I said to the whipper-snapper who waited for me to hand him the invitation. "I was invited to the Cramer-Sinclair wedding, but I forgot to bring the invitation."

He gave me a look that said, Oh sure, mister. A likely story!"

"Call 'em; they'll tell you," I pleaded.

He just spread his arms wide and looked at me..

"Okay," I said, "I'm really here to capture the bride and carry her away for myself. I can't do that if you don't park my car and let me in." Actually, it sounded like a great plan to me.

The kid reached out and opened my car door. Good grief, I got away with a story and didn't even have to bribe the guy. As I stepped out on the asphalt, the kid held out his hand. Damn, a trip, not a bribe. I fished in my pocket and pulled out an unseen bill. As he snatched it away from me, I realized it was a tenner. *A fiver would have done it, Jake,* I said to myself. Ah well, I just hoped the drinks inside were free.

The ballroom was on the second floor. I took the elevator with several other people. The cage had full-length mirrors. I tried to look blasé as I turned sideways to look at myself. Double damn if I didn't look pretty doggone good! I hadn't seen myself look this good since . . . well, since never. I stood up tall as I got off the elevator.

"Jaaake!" a loud voice said. Yeah, it was Cora Lee in a lavender dress. She looked like an angel.

She ran up and hugged one of my legs. "Hey," I said, "you're wrinkling my suit!"

She backed up and smoothed both hands over the material and said, "Sorry, Jake. I'm just *so* glad to see you." Then she stood back, pinched her dress at each side and said, "Don't I look great?"

"No, you look super, super great!"

"I gotta go," she said. "Mama's almost ready, and I have to go up between the chairs with Donna even before Mama goes up to meet Carl. See you after."

I found a seat among the other guests. There were a lot of them. Cramer must have had lots of family and friends. Rhodes wasn't there and neither was Cramer's ex-wife. But Jake Whitter was. I felt a little like the father of the bride and maybe the uncle of a short, sassy little bridesmaid.

A side door opened and a man in a clerical robe came out with Cramer and another man. They walked to position themselves under the flower-covered gazebo up front. Then music filled the room. Everyone else stood up, so I did too. They turned around, so I did too. I saw Donna, all in lavender, come from the back of the chairs, and everyone smiled, so I did too. Next came a little bundle of lavender with flowers in her hair. Cora Lee. "Ah," everyone said, so I did too.

I don't remember much about the wedding ceremony. I remember promises and "I do's." I remember a beautiful Loretta looking with worship at Cramer. I remember Cramer looking so proud. I remember the new couple going back down the center aisle together. I remember Cora Lee having a smile that would crack the moon. Two tissues in my pocket weren't enough.

I followed the crowd up some stairs to a balcony with tables covered with white cloths and with an indecent amount of food. But then I am an indecent sort of fellow. I wanted to grab a plate immediately, but I just stood and made choices in my mind first. I watched what others did.

"You like shrimp?" a voice said beside me. I looked up to see a blue dress with a red scarf. It was covering a lady — definitely a lady, not just a woman—who had more age marks in her face than a road map.

"No," I said, "shrimp decided one day that they didn't like me, so I ignore them for revenge."

She laughed and held out a hand. "I'm Sarah," she said.

I grabbed the hand and said, "Jake Whittaker."

"Can I fix you a plate? I imagine that meat and cheese might be right up your alley."

"How did you know I eat in the alley? Thanks, but I'll just grab whatever looks good."

"Okay, but how about sitting over there with me and telling me about how you know Loretta and Carl?"

When we sat down with full plates — at least mine was — I said, "I met Cora Lee first."

"That cute little bridesmaid? She looked so proud of her mother."

"There's no one like Loretta. Carl's lucky."

"Yes," she said. "Carl's my son, but he didn't come into my life until I was almost forty. He's the love of my life." He was married before to someone who didn't want to be second fiddle to Carl's business."

"Will that be Loretta's life also?"

"I doubt that with Loretta. And certainty not with little Cora Lee. That one doesn't take second fiddle to anything or anyone!"

Yeah. If Cora Lee likes something, she gives it her full attention and expects the same back.

And suddenly, there she was, changed into a pink dress and shiny shoes.

"Jake! Mama Cramer! Did you just love the wedding? Did you, did you?"

"Loved it!" Sarah and I both said at once.

Cora Lee looked at Sarah Cramer and said, "Mama Cramer, can I steal Jake for a little bit? Mama said it's okay." She took my hand and started pulling me toward the stairs. Sarah looked over at Loretta, got a wave from Loretta like it was okay, and Cora Lee grabbed my hand.

"Where are we going? Where are you taking me?" I asked.

She didn't stop. She smiled and tugged me along. "We're gonna go to that Melissa's wedding. Mama said we could 'check in' to that other wedding, but we need to hurry back. Come on, maybe we'll be in time for the food they have there."

Wouldn't you know it, we got the same valet parking kid I'd had coming in. I handed Cora Lee the parking ticket and said, "You get my car."

The kid looked at the ticket, looked at Cora Lee, looked at me, and said, "This the bride?" When I didn't answer, he said, "You steal the kid? Should I call the police?"

"I'm not a kid!" Cora Lee shouted at him. "I'm a bridesmaid, and my Mama said I can go with Jake, so go get the car!"

Eyebrows went up. The parking kid looked at me, I just put a "so there" look on my face.

The car showed up three minutes later. This time I only tipped a buck.

★★★

The parking at Dabbling Park was "find your own place if you can." I did.

"Hurry, Jake, hurry. I hear music."

We walked into the chapel at Dabbling Park to see Melissa and Mally walking over to some tables near a large grill. They were followed by Mrs. Geraldine Duck. Of course.

Ah Melissa. A vision in white. The dress hugged her hips and opened up by her ankles. I think I would have drooled if Cora Lee hadn't been there. Mally had a happy face. Geraldine Duck had a determined face. My face must have been a little sad.

"There she is!" Cora Lee shouted. Then damn if she didn't hightail right over there. "Melissa, Melissa," Cora Lee said, before I could catch up and stop her.

Melissa looked at Cora Lee with a puzzled look. "Who..." she began.

"I'm Cora Lee. I was with Jake, Jake Whittaker, the day he told you where your bird was. Remember?"

"Oh yeah. Glad to see you again Cora Lee. Where's Jake?"

"Here," I said. "You look so, so lovely, Melissa."

Geraldine Duck, standing behind Mally said, "Mr. Whittaker, you didn't acknowledge you were coming to this welding. Did you think you could just show up?"

"I was invited."

"You didn't acknowledge that you would attend."

When I said nothing, she looked at Cora Lee and said, "And who is this?"

I grabbed Cora Lee's hand and said, "This is Cora Lee Sinclair. She's a friend of mine and my guest to this wedding. Surely you assumed that if I'm invited I can bring a guest. Cora Lee is my guest."

Cora Lee stood there dumbfounded. She didn't understand the ins and outs of adult relationships. Loretta had taught her only the "ins," where everyone is "in" and of value. Meanwhile, Melissa stared at her new mother-in-law.

Geraldine's head shot up with arrogance and authority. "You can't be here. You didn't respond."

I looked at Melissa with a question on my face. It was time to see if she was going to be under Geraldine's thumb in this new marriage. Melissa shifted on one foot, bringing a hip up that accented the curve of her body. I wet my lips. Then Melissa cleared her throat and half-whispered, "Jake—Mr. Whittaker—is my guest." In a louder voice, she said, "Mama Duck, this is Mally's and my wedding, and *Jake* is welcome here." She looked at Cora Lee and added, "His guest is most welcome, too." Cora Lee grinned at her.

Yea, Melissa. It won't be easy, but you're going to make a place for yourself in your new family.

Geraldine stared at Melissa and then turned to show us her ridged back as she walked away.

Melissa smiled at me. She smiled at Cora Lee, grabbed Cora Lee's hand and walked her away saying, "Come on, Sweetheart, let's go get some food.

Oh yeah, Melissa gets away with calling her Sweetheart! But who cares anyway.

I looked at Mally for the first time, wagged my head and said, "I guess we can follow those two. What'd you say?"

Mally and I joined the ladies at the bullet table.

For about thirty minutes Cora Lee and I picked up goodies to eat from little plates that were almost too small to be called plates. Cheapskate Geraldine!

"We gotta go, Jake," Cora Lee finally said. "Mama's gonna wonder what happened to us."

"Okay. Gimme a second." I went over to Melissa, wrapped my arms around her shoulders, kissed her, and said, "Thanks, Beautiful One. Have a great marriage."

She kissed me back, and I floated out of there with what I imagine was a wondrous smile on my face. I couldn't stop sighing.

★★★

"Cora Lee!" Loretta shouted. "I thought you two got lost. I was worried about you."

"No, Mama. We saw Mrs. . . ."

"Mrs. Duck," I added for her.

"We saw her in her wedding dress almost as nice as yours, Mama. We saw a Mr. Mally who married her. We saw Mally's Mama who wasn't very nice. We . . . we would rather be here, huh, Jake?"

"You bet, Sweetheart." I'd said it again. The evil look was back. Gee, kids are so unpredictable.

★★★

By the end of the afternoon, Loretta handed Cora Lee off to Donna. As I watched them join hands, I felt . . . like going home to my office with my pillow and blanket on the couch.

I guess it's a good thing that I don't like kids, especially eight-year-olds who have a stubborn streak. At least I think so.

Back at the office, I hit the couch and plopped the pillow under my head. I felt alone. I needed to kick some ass. Mine.

Just then the phone rang. Maybe it's a new client with new places to go, new people to see, new problems to solve...

Maybe it's Cora Lee.

Made in the USA
Monee, IL
04 June 2020